THE HERE AND NOW

a novel by

Anthony D. Carr

ACARRA Publishing

ACARRA Publishing
5 East Superior
Chicago, Il 60611

Manufactured in the United States of America

Library of Congress Cataloging-in-publication Data is available

ISBN 0-970-77610-1

For information regarding special discounts or bulk purchases, please call 312.217.5254

To e-mail the author write to tonycarr50@hotmail.com

To the friends and lovers allover the world
May you have the strength to stay friends and
lovers throughout time.

Prologue
What's up with Dee?

At year thirty-six, De Acquinn Carter is at his best and his worst. Standing straight and towering, his five-foot eight-inch frame commands the respect of one much taller. Over the years, he has learned that what is often assumed of a taller man has to be earned by someone his height. It is earned through demeanor, attitude, certitude, and just a slight hint of playfulness that takes the edge off a driving style. That small hint of playfulness allows one to endear themselves to this man. Once comfortable, most call him Dee. The others he lets struggle with the enunciation of De Acquinn.

Standing with three by his side, clearly there is nothing that is going to detract from this mission. Boys rehearse their entire lives for this very moment; the moment when strength of character defines how one handles the unknown.

It is amazing how little boys in America can grow into men with no father by their sides. Longing for the essence of what makes a man a man, they grow up clinging to whatever vestiges of masculinity they can emulate. Too often, what they pick up goes untenured by the love that a father can provide. A father's love can be sometimes demanding, sometimes tenderhearted, and many times seemingly unsympathetic. However, a father always inside, cares too much but that father understands that not being liked at this moment by a child does not mean that you are unloved.

It is nurturing that only the day-to-day interaction with a caring father figure can provide. He should be able to provide the refining that grooms a boy into a young man. He also provides the groundwork that furnishes support for that young man to build the foundation of manhood on.

At this defining moment in my life, the years of building from young adulthood to manhood beam from me. It's a feeling that is empowering and draining at the same time. One of the lucky ones, my dad, Frank, was with me until just before I turned eight. Then, the unthinkable happened – he was snatched from my life. At that slice in time, it was questionable whether the footing that had been built would support my uncertain life ahead.

* * *

I hate the smell of this place. Well, just one last check-up and we're on. Everything is so sterile. I look down at my watch and notice that they are late. At that same moment the lifting of my arm reminds me that my back is killing me. I need one of those Grace back rubs right now. One ten-minute back rub from Grace and you are relaxed and ready to deal with anything.

I met Grace as a second semester freshman at Northern Illinois University just before I pledged Alpha Phi Alpha. Back when I was still one of the nicest young men in the world. It was before I was turned out; it was Grace and Dee. Her voice was like music to my ears. Just the sound of it filled me with anticipation of the relaxation that was about to follow. It was not the sex. Sex was something that we got around to when we got around to it.

Grace was four years older than I was. She was able to fill voids that no amount of sex could. She found me when I needed a lot of love. Her way instantly touched me and made me know that I was loved. It was a time when I needed all of the love the world could offer.

As a child I didn't have it. It's not as if I did not grow up in a loving family. It's just that in our house, love was never openly shown. It was so concealed that the first hug that I can recall was not from my mother but from my second grade teacher, Miss Sardonie. For some reason she took a liking to a short little boy that came to school in tattered clothes. It was the day that she hugged me close to her bosom that I fell in love with the touch of a woman.

From that moment on, I fell for all women. Their touch, their smell, their mannerisms -

females as a whole body of work. A work that could erase all of the days of isolation from not feeling loved as a child. A body of work that provides the reassurance that the best is always yet to come.

Grace's reassurance, not unlike that second-grade reassuring hug, replenished me for the ongoing journey. Everybody needs physical reassurance. It does not have to be sexual in nature – just physical. We are no different from the other primates that use touch as a means to bond. Look at how many animals groom each other. Think about how great it feels to just have someone wash and style your hair. Am I right, or am I right?

Grace was very sexy. She is what my grandfather would call "high yellow." Grace, despite her age, is the kind of woman who has a full meal waiting for you if she knows that you're coming. She is ready to sit in silence or have a full conversation.

To this day, I don't know if we just vibed that way or if it was just her way. She was the first in a long line of women that I should have paid more attention to but didn't. Each time it came to pass that you don't miss your water until your well runs dry. She had the first set of D-cups that I had ever seen. She was small and tight everywhere else. She just had not grown into her chest yet. Looking at her fully clothed you wouldn't know that she was hiding those things. She kept her chest cinched down tight with what she called "good bras." The bras were not very pleasing to the eye. No lace - just support.

Our time was filled with candles, back rubs, reading from erotic books, and frank conversations. I could talk to her about anything. She was truly my friend and lover.

Grace was my first. Not my first sexual partner but clearly, my first partner - the first woman to give herself completely. The first woman to care enough to teach me "how to" – how to dress, how to buy quality clothes, how to pick out quality restaurants, how to use credit, how to dream.

What I was getting from her was insight and knowledge to last a lifetime. I never said thank you. Our second summer we just drifted apart. I guess we had come about as far as a relationship with a nineteen-year-old "boy" could go. It was time to put up or shut-up. I was still too immature to do either.

Understanding what she was to me, I grieved when I realized she was gone. Not the type of grief that comes with the loss of someone you love. The grief that overcomes you when you lose a friend when there is nothing and no one to fill the space that has been abandoned by the loss; not a friend, parent, or any other woman. Call it funny or call it sad but I knew in my heart the moment that she left me.

Still friends, the relationship quietly passed from a "no holds barred" interaction to one that was guarded. It passed to a point where two people love each other but will never give of themselves completely for fear of having one's heart broken into ten pieces. Ten pieces hurts.

Having lost the one I would most like to talk to, I found that the only peace that I could find was expressing myself to Grace. Grace not taking my calls left me with one choice; write her a letter. It is a letter that she has never seen.

March 21

My Dearest Grace,

Clearly, I don't have the words to tell you what you mean to me. If the words had come, you would be mine and be with me now. I feel abandoned - a ship out to sea with a storm approaching and the entire crew is dead. As dead as the place in my heart that wants you to revive it. Darling, I am truly lost without you. What hurts the most is that you won't talk to me. I don't know what went wrong. Please call.

Hugs and kisses from your Dee.

Till next time.

Dee

The letter being written, I was able to put my mind to rest.

Chapter 1
Lets Go To Vegas Boys

Where did this neck and back pain come from anyway? I haven't even gotten on the plane yet. It's a fast plane to Las Vegas for me and my boys a last minute unplanned getaway of sorts. My crew includes my friends Len Edwards, Daryl Black, and Albert Gold. All I had to say was we're going to Vegas boys, everyone either got off work, got sick at work all of a sudden, or would think of some great excuse for skipping work once we got there. The trip was for three days of fun and frolic culminating with a fourth day of taking care of business.

As usual, Daryl was at the airport early. We were flying American Airlines out of O'Hare Airport. Domestic reservationists will always tell you to be at the airport a couple of hours early. For Daryl, this translated to being three hours early. Me, I hate waiting. I generally get to the gate about twenty minutes early – just before they release your confirmed seat assignment. It also gives you enough time to check for plane delays while en route to the airport.

When checking on the status of your flight, don't just ask the ticket agent if the plane is on time or not? Doing that only gives you some of the picture. You should also ask the agent about the status of the equipment, the airplane. Where is the plane right now?

It's a fair bet that if the plane is still en route to the airport, your flight is not going to leave until at least twenty minutes after the plane lands.

I stroll up to the gate without a care in the world. I spied Daryl's three hundred fifty pounds sweating bullets. I don't need a bunch of trauma this early on a Wednesday so I take the offensive and yell out, "Hey I've got the tickets."

A number of years ago, I met Daryl at work. After being in the field for seven months as a consultant, I came into the office one day and Daryl acted like he was my best friend. Normally, I am very standoffish with new people and even more so with men. Most men want to get into your video to see what you are doing and start trouble. What's more, believe it or not, many men are as jealous and vindictive as any woman could ever be. If your woman is fine, they want to know what you have that they don't. If your car is live, they put themselves in debt trying to get a better one. The list goes on and on.

Think about it, if you hear about trouble, most times it is between or about men. My grandfather told me, before I was old enough to understand, that if you have three true friends during your lifetime you will be lucky. With Daryl it was easy; I knew what he wanted. He wanted to get to the field where the money and action were. The difference is twice the take-home pay for the same work, more client interface, and if you're good, a fast track to management. This made Daryl a good friend right from the start.

I helped Daryl out. He was not a threat to me or my current rise at the company. As repayment, I received a friend whether I wanted one or not. Don't get me wrong; I am better off having him as a friend. Just like our approaches to flying, our personalities are one hundred and eighty degrees apart. With his very conservative and idealistic views on life, he provides a great sounding board for all of the crazy things that I have going on in my life. I walked up to Daryl and gave him a big hearty "what's up" with a hug. I tell him that "it's on." The hug takes a lot out of me.

Daryl, at just under six feet, clearly underestimates his natural strength. He literally hugs the air right out of my lungs. While doing so, he asks me in my ear, "Have you spoken with Charity?"

I just put up my hand and told him, “We'll talk." Just what I needed – a downer at a time like this. I walked over to the check-in counter and quickly insured that our upgrades to first class have gone through and that my seat is as far away from them as possible. I'm with my best friends and I want to be by myself.

Over the years, I have averaged flying at least one day out of the week since I graduated from college. Back in coach I find myself from the time we take off, counting the minutes until we land. Going mostly from Chicago to Dallas - Ft. Worth, I would try to fly at the same time with flight attendants that are familiar with me.

A crowded plane many times means a free upgrade to first class for me. I also have a relationship with a special check-in agent who takes care of me. I would see her when I could and I always gave her what she needed, being mostly great sex since her boyfriend wasn't quit gifted in that department. In return she routinely finds me on the flight manifest. Just like magic, I am in first class. It's true, better-looking people get breaks. It also doesn't hurt to have your gear going on so that they know that there's some real substance behind the face.

Anyway, the powers that be got us into first class. For using my influence, my boys think that I am a demigod. All the time my insides tell of my mortality.

First class boards first. It's a big plane - a 747. I am on the other side of first class from my boys. Len comes over and asks what am I doing way over here. I tell him a white lie that my seat got messed up and I couldn't change it. With this being his first time on a plane, anything that I say about flying goes without question. Off he goes back to his seat and though I should not be, I am relieved.

Before I could get my bags situated, the flight attendant is calling my name and asking if I want her to take my coat. Oh, the joys of first class. I have on a lightweight trench that needs to be hung that I give to her. I settle into my seat and the curse that Daryl laid on me starts to take hold. I start to think about Charity. I reminisce as I drift off into a dream like state.

It all started one Sunday when Daryl suggested that I visit his church, New Hope Baptist Church. The church was a new venture, so the service was being held in the auditorium of Lindblom Technical High School.

Everything about the service was tacky except the message from the pastor. The message was about finding your direction in life by listening to God. The message was that most of us spend too much time telling God how great He is and not listening to what He is saying to us. The message was so good that my donation was large.

After the service, I waited around to meet the reverend Paul Usher. I was told that we had something in common - we are both in the same fraternity, Alpha Phi Alpha. While waiting, I was approached by a young lady who wanted to know if I wanted to join the church's singles ministry. Clearly, I didn't and I said so. The forward young lady had the gall to ask why.

Thinking quickly on my feet, I responded that I did not want to get a bunch of junk in the mail. She was in the process of telling me that I would not get any junk mail when Daryl came over and introduced me to the young lady.

Her name was Charity Johnson. Her intentions were clear. Without an ulterior motive, my negative reply to not wanting to join the singles ministry would have sent her away. After being introduced to Charity, I felt at ease to play with her motives.

I quickly apologized for giving her a hard time about the singles ministry and offered to make it up to her over lunch one day. She took the bait hook, line, and sinker. She pulled out one of the singles ministry's sign up cards and filled it out and handed it to me. The card included everything except her measurements - I could guess those.

Charity was brown skin with a Halle Berry hairdo. Slim in the waist, big in the butt - thirty-eight across the hips, small chested - about a 32B. She had on a simple blue dress that showed off her fitness. The most attractive thing about her was her light brown eyes that were encased in a pair of slanted eye sockets.

The entire package was interesting. Not the show stopping presentation that I was used to, but not bad for something to do. I responded to her offer of the card with a simple "I'll stay in touch."

Her smile said, "You do that." The encounter was over and as quick as it happened, it was forgotten. The card with her information was shoved deep into my breast pocket only to be retrieved by the dry cleaner before its deep blue ink could ruin my jacket.

Charity, being reduced to a distant memory, faded with the everyday toils of consulting in the nuclear power industry. Everyday there is a new hot issue that has to be solved within the specified time or the utility has to shut the power plant down. Between the loss of revenue from the plant and the purchase of replacement power, the shutdown of a unit can cost millions of dollars per day. The stakes are high.

Being the only Black person doing what I do, and people being people, any decision that costs the client money is hotly contested – contested by the very company I work for as well as the client. To stay employed, there is no room for error. It takes a strong brother to stand his ground and do what's right. There is a lot at stake.

Respect is the name of the game. It keeps you employed and cuts down on the number of heated battles. Either way, by the end of the week, you are drained. Any thoughts one might have of calling that slant-eyed woman faded, and the need for self- preservation prevailed.

After a particularly hard work week, three weeks later, I found my way back to New Hope for the message. At the end of the service, I saw Charity and immediately went into a song and dance about being too busy to keep our lunch date. Then came the "If you give me your number again maybe we can do it this week as a dinner." After letting me squirm a few minutes, she gave me the number again. This time I would call.

* * *

Our date began with Charity meeting me downtown at my office in the south loop on Polk Street. We meet around eight o'clock on Saturday. She was dressed for a casual night on the town - jeans and a black cashmere sweater. Her five-foot one-inch frame is enriched by a pair of black one and a half inch heeled sandals. Her toes were perfect. Pretty feet are always a plus.

It's working. She has a certain savoir-faire that keeps drawing me in deeper. It's clear that there is more to this church girl than meets the eye. Her way sparks each of your senses while disarming you, daring you to give her more of a chance. We decided to have Chinese food for dinner. Chinatown is not far away from my office so we decide to go there.

We get into my Mazda Millenia S. It has a fresh coat of wax on its pearl white finish thanks to a complete detail by my main man Eyes. Eyes has been doing my car for about two years. He works at "The Last Detail" over on Clark Street. I pull in and very few words are required. He knows what I want; he just has to know how much time he has to do it. Today, I wanted a good job so I don't rush him. This kind of service is standard for me.

There are two main ingredients that go into service. First I establish myself as one outside of the rank and file that frequent the business. There are many ways to do this. Always flash a smile - no one wants to be around a grouch.

Compliment, compliment, compliment. A good, well placed compliment brightens anyone's day. It makes them feel good. Make statements that are going to get you remembered. Statements that you can refer to in the future to make the person remember you. In a big city, having places that you control is a must. It sets me apart and provides status. Of course the most important thing to remember, if a tip is warranted, make it a good one. Tipping when a tip is not expected will get you noticed even if the tip is declined.

A ten-dollar drink at your favorite bar may warrant a ten-dollar tip. Even if the next drink is not on the house, the service when you're trying to impress the woman that you're talking to will be prompt and the pour much better. Being a good tipper, I will tip ten dollars or more to Eyes, an amount more than most people pay for a car wash. You get what you pay and tip for. If the guy knows that the tip is coming, he will give you that value before the tip is paid.

In the car, the conversation is slow. I have Sade, crooning in the background setting the mood. I pull into the parking lot on Cermak Road and park the car. It's a short walk over to the spot, Emperors Choice. I've been coming here for years. The food is outstanding. It's a little later in the evening so there should not be a wait for a table.

I open the door to a greeting of "Dcarter" in a heavy accent. The smiles are wide and the emotion from the greeter is clearly genuine. It pays to have places that you feel at home. I eat here at least once a week when I am in town. I look over to Charity to see if she is impressed. Like kisses, eyes don't lie. It's working. We are seated and handed menus. I ask Charity if she wants to be adventurous and let me order for her. She flashes her million dollar eyes at me and gives me an affirmative.

"Do you like spicy food?" I ask while the waiter stands over us.

"Oh, I love spicy food." She replies to my delight.

Not needing a menu, I tell the waiter that we will have the General's Shrimp, Singapore Noodles, and Shrimp Fried Rice, extra spicy. It's a lot of food and I already know that the leftovers will be great tomorrow.

The lighting in the room is dim which sets a mood for light conversation. The food arrives and we eat over our conversation. Minute by minute, word by word, smile by smile, I'm feeling it more and more. It's as if this was meant to be and all I have to do is flow with it. It's all good.

I get the parking ticket validated and we leave under the cover of a light rain. Feeling with my heart, the essence of the moment mandates that I touch Charity. I calmly slip my hand into hers. I don't know if she knew that my heart was in that hand.

Staying in my element, we go over to the 95 Club on the 95th floor of the John Hancock Building on the city's Gold Coast. As soon as we get off the elevator, Alex, a long time employee of the bar, notices me. I shake his hand and exchange a concealed five-dollar bill with him.

The small sum gets a table at the w overlooking a south view of the Loop, Navy Pie and Lake Michigan. The view is breathtaking. Charity is from the western suburbs of Chicago and does not get downtown often. The excitement flowing from her is worth the price of admission.

We get settled in oversized chairs that are meant to make you comfortable enough so that the thought of leaving vanishes. This allows the bar to serve more drinks. I ordered a Glenlivet on the rocks and Charity ordered Tanquerray with Rose's lime juice. I was surprised and impressed with her drink order. This woman takes her drinking seriously. There were brief moments of intense conversation but most of the time was spent just looking out over the city. There were some stories about things that we did in the places that we could spot from our perch high atop the building intermixed with the clouds. Then it hit me; all of the moments of silence between us were comfortable. At that time, I knew that I really liked this girl.

Charity's car is parked outside of my office so we head back that way. When we get to her car, I don't want the night to end. I ask her if she would like to come up and see my office. My office is about seven hundred square feet; just enough room for a small waiting area in front, an assistant's station, and my office in the back, away from everything.

Everything in the office, from the telephones to the lighting, is ultramodern. You can't charge clients one hundred fifty dollars an hour and have an office that says that the client is overpaying. Since I spend so much time in the office, my office has all the comforts of home. Large screen television with satellite and DVD, a wardrobe that is stocked with workout gear, and two complete changes of clothes, a CD player with about three hundred CDs, a small fridge, my desk, a couch, and of course a shit load of work.

We get upstairs into the office and I offer her a bottle of LeCroix mineral water as I put the leftover Chinese food into the fridge. I pour the water into a champagne glass - remembering that presentation is everything - I pop in a DVD and sit next to Charity on the couch.

Not one to take a chance on a surprise this early in a friendship, I asked the question before taking any action. A simple softly spoken, "Can I kiss you?" The answer is less important than the response you get from her body language. The answer I received included her body relaxing in my arms and the moment proceeding uninterrupted.

The shaking of her head indicating yes was a foregone conclusion that her actions had revealed. I lightly brush her lips with mine. I outline her lips by lightly tracing them with the tip of my tongue. A slight inhaling through my lips while they cover hers evaporates any moisture that was deposited there. I gently kiss both corners of her mouth, give a cotton-like suck on her bottom lip that is followed by a soft bite. The kiss is finished with a covering of her lips with mine and my tongue inserted into her mouth just enough to taste her. The sensations to her lips all happen in about seven seconds. My first kiss sets me apart from most others and sets the tone for all other sexual interaction.

With no thought of the emotional consequences, her black sweater was off. I paused to admire the black lacy camisole that was underneath her sweater. The sheer fabric just hid a chest that required no support. A woman who has her underwear in order turns me on. Bras and panties that don't match, the wrong kind of bra for the outfit, or just plain raggedy underwear lets you know something about the woman.

If a woman takes care in the things that only she and those closest to her will see, then it is a fair bet that she cares enough about herself to want and give the best of herself in other aspects of her life - hopefully to you too. Not to mention that it's sexy as hell. Charity's unzipped pants revealed panties that matched the camisole. If it's at all possible, I am falling deeper just by the sight of this partially clothed woman and I'm not doing anything to stop it.

The next two hours were filled with the joy of exploring. She smelled good allover. Her response to my touch, my soft kisses and gentle whispers made me feel like I had found my queen. There was nothing that I was going to do to mess this up. So I pulled back and held her in my arms at arms length. I asked her if she was comfortable. She replied with a smile. I buried my head into her.

Several hours later we smell like each other. I smelled like Charity and she me. Still not wanting things to end, we held onto each other, half asleep and half awake, until the morning sun crept through the windowpane. A bond was forged without one word of why or one thought of how come. As crazy as it sounds, it just happened.

* * *

Finally alone, the light from the television cast shadows across the room that settled our feelings. There was a slight thrill of being alone with him for the first time. Dee started to undress me. I looked away and acted a little shy while all the time wanting to see everything that was transpiring. Having been in this situation once or twice before, it was still amazing how typical men were in their desire that the woman be innocent. The shy look away always had an effect on a man.

We were lying on the couch while the light from the television made flickering designs on the walls of the room in a rhythm that was slightly like the beating of my heart. My heart was racing like this was the first time.

Lying in his arms on the couch in his office, for some reason, my reactions to his soft touches were filled with nervous anticipation. He must have sensed my physical state - his touch was so slow, his kisses so caring. His actions opened every pore of my soul and I found myself giving all of me to him.

After having brought me to this point, he asks me this stupid question, "Can I kiss you?"

Do bees buzz? Do dogs bark? Man, if you don't stop all of this bull shit and get your tongue in my mouth... Playing my coy roll to the hilt, I politely said "yes." What I meant to say was, "what's taking you so long?"

He sat me in a sitting position and for a moment, I could feel his eyes admiring me. Still in my panties and camisole, the look on his face was that of a world-renowned painter looking at a subject that would forever be embedded on the canvas of his memory. It was sexy and scary at the same time.

It's hard to believe at twenty-five that I had never been kissed just so; never had I been touched just so; never had the anticipation of what was to come taken over my actions. We were in concert and going somewhere I had never been. Should I run from this place? I can feel my heart for the first time in my life. It is a pounding that asks for this instant to never end. Like a virgin, giving completely of herself for the first time, I will never be the same again.

Like a dancer on a ballroom floor, I began responding to Dee's every move. A force outside of me arched my back forcing my breasts to scream in the most unladylike manner- "touch me." Okay, Dee responded by cupping them - first like newborn kittens, then firm like he was ensuring that he had found the sweetest, juiciest plums in the bin, and finally with a flickering of his tongue. Dee put all three actions together and confirmed an ability to read me - heart, body and soul. Through it all, the word that stands out most is "darling."

As the word darling was spoken by Dee, it echoed through me and made me feel sexy. Before he bore his full weight onto me, his full size into me, I was prepped by the most skillful licking. Concentrating in just the right spots, it brought me to a point where I lost control of myself. Just as he was stopping, I felt a little bit of me escape onto the couch. That had never happen before and it took me by surprise. I instinctively pushed him away from my pulsating intersection.

Facing me, he began a pushing - "My Darling" - that began the process of forcing the essence of all others that had come before him out of my soul. It was a cleansing of the spirit that allowed what was next to be. Rising up onto his arms we pushed ourselves into one. Rocking a world of old memories from me with the sweat that was dripping from my pores to be replaced by the substance of a newfound love. Rocking and rocking and rocking until all that remained was one. The one had no name. It took the form of love.

"Oh, darling," were the words that Dee said over and over to me.

"Yes?"

"Oh, darling"

"Yes?"

He rocked me ever so slowly. Tightly engulfed in his arms, he commanded, "Mine."

"Get it all baby - it's all yours."

"Yes, baby?" I uttered as our bodies in concert moved at the same beat as my heart.

"Is that it darling?"

"Yes, that's it. That's... Oh, Oh... I come baby..."

The sensation being new, I shifted quickly and tried to catch my body as it shifted uncontrollably. In Dee's arms, I calm down my body and mind.

Throughout the night, love had been made, passions exchanged and love made again and again. As the sun crept through the blinded windowpanes, I knew my life would never be the same.

Chapter 2
First Class

"To drink? I'll have a Glenlivet on the rocks."

"I'm sorry, Mr. Carter we didn't stock Glenlivet for the flight. How about some Black Label? ," she suggested.

It's not really my drink but at twenty thousand feet you take what they have and you are grateful to have it. "Yes, that will be fine," I replied. "How long is the flight?"

"It's going to be about four hours. Do you want some warm nuts?," she inquired, obviously trying to take my mind off the length of the flight. The flight attendant's name is Nancy. I had flown with her on several occasions in the past, back in coach. I think she remembers a conversation I had with her about my flying too much and it starting to wear on me.

Most non-business people, when they go to the airport, are in a good mood. They are either going somewhere fun or picking up someone that they want to see. For the business traveler, it becomes a routine that places you in a confined space, with stale air, marginal provisions and what seems like people always talking too loud. Sounds like fun, huh?

The scotch was served in a glass that was equivalent to the best glass in my office bar. Oh, the wonders of first class. If I were back in coach, I would be drinking out of a plastic cup right now and with my luck probably sitting in front of a crying baby. A mixture of warm nuts followed. Soon thereafter, Nancy was asking if I wanted salmon or the steak for my meal.

With my issues, being healthy is job one so I order the salmon. The meal starts with Nancy taking the cup of nuts away and spreading a blue oversized napkin over the tray table. A small garden salad is served with a choice of dressings.

There are three flight attendants working first class for the flight so the service is excellent. Nancy notices that the two airplane bottles of scotch have evaporated from my glass and within seconds she is asking me if I would like a refill. I nibble on the salad that I have ordered with creamy garlic dressing. As it is taken away, the main entree is served.

Real plates are used - not some microwave safe dish that has all the food crammed into it in a way that makes it impossible to ascertain what is in the dish. Your choice of the type of roll and you are asked if you would like some red or white wine. Of course I stick with the Black Label. Having no appetite, I do more playing with the food than eating it.

Nancy comes over and inquires if everything is okay with the food. Being truthful with her I tell her, "Nancy my stomach is upset and I probably couldn't keep it down if I ate it."

"That's too bad. Then you probably won't be interested in the sundaes that we have for you guys?" she questioned.

Being a kid at heart and knowing that American's sundaes are made with some of the best ice cream and topped with whatever you like, I could not pass it up. "Are you crazy? I'll have one with lots of caramel, whipped topping, and a cherry. No nuts now," I caution pointing to my stomach. Nancy just smiled and went back to her duties.

When the sundae is served, I can't help but wonder how they have room for all of the food that they carry on a plane. I eat every last bit of the ice cream. Just as I am finishing it, the in-flight movie begins. I search the seat back in front of me for the barf bag. I think I am going to pay for my indulgence. Oh well, a small price to pay. I just hate wasting the good scotch. Maybe I'll be okay.

The typical first class flyers are deep within themselves during the flight. They are focused on their day's activities or catching up with what tomorrow will bring. There are a few first class passengers that are truly enjoying the flight; they must be the ultra wealthy or tourists. One thing that they have in common is money to burn, either theirs or someone elses.

Most first class passengers are not exposed to people of color taking part in an activity that is priced to exclude. You can read it in their faces. It is as if a black person is trying to gain admission, just for the day, mind you, to an exclusive all white country club. From time to time one is bold enough to ask, "What is it that you do?" Their interest peaked by the splash of color in the first class cabin. Today, with four thirty-something black men in their mist, it would be to good to be true not to be approached by one of the elite.

The question starts off simple enough, "Where are you guys going?" asks a fortyish woman sitting across the aisle.

Clearly we are all on our way to Las Vegas; it's a fact that I politely don't point out to her. I simply answer her question with the obvious answer and brace for what I know is next. In this arena we are truly representing the entire race.

The conversation proceeds and just when I think that things are going to be different this time, she asks what must have been burning inside of her during the flight, "What's the name of the group?"

Really not getting where she is coming from, my reply is, "Pardon me."

Sensing that she had crossed a line, she goes into an apology intermixed with a rephrasing of her question that is totally incomprehensible but for the fact that I have been down this road before.

Minding my manners, I let her off easy. I begin to explain that we are not part of a singing group but are actually part of a consortium that has started mining for silver in Nevada. With our initial efforts having been positive, we are on our way to the mine to tour it and finalize expansion plans.

Caught off guard, my tongue-in-cheek comments are followed by an "Oh my gush" from her lips. With no other conversation coming from her, I see her slump back into her seat and start to ponder. I can only guess that she is trying to reevaluate those old wives tales that she might have heard about black people. She must reconcile this exchange so that she does not have to change her entire way of thinking about blacks. Me? I'm just happy to have dodged another bullet and only hope that the white lie has done its job well.

***

Before you know it the in-flight movie is over and its time to land. I made it and I still have my scotch in me. We exit the plane and make our way to the baggage claim area. Not liking to spend more time in an airport then I need to, I always pack light. Unless I am going overseas or I just have to, I don't check my luggage. As everyone else is fighting to get their luggage, I have a seat knowing the retrieving of their luggage will take at least twenty minutes.

Watching, I notice a limo driver searching the baggage area holding up a sign with "Carter" printed in large letters across it. The limo is compliments of the hotel. In no hurry, I watch the driver and am not surprised to see him completely ignore me and wave his card in front of every white man's face. I let him go on like that for about a minute or two before I walk up to him. When I do, the look on his face is a real Kodak moment.

The man who has our baggage is an expert at negotiating from the baggage area out to the limo. At the limo the driver took charge and the bags were loaded in no time flat.

In scant moments we're pulling away from the airport in a white full stretch Lincoln on our way to the Flamingo Hilton Hotel on the Strip. Outside it was very hot so I was glad to be under the car's forceful air conditioning unit. I sit back and enjoy the ride.

During the ride, Len and Daryl's eyes are glued to the limo's car windows as we pass sites that they have only seen in the movies and on television. Al and I are Vegas veterans so the sites are nothing new to us.

Unlike Vegas cab drivers that will give you an explanation of everything going on in town and explain the sites and new construction, limo drivers are all business. Seeing the wonder in Len and Daryl's eyes, Al sits up on the edge of his seat and starts pointing out places of interest that we are passing. He points out the Hard Rock, Baileys, MGM Grand, and Ceasers among other places.

We arrive at the Flamingo. The limo driver and bellhop retrieve our bags. I tip the driver a twenty and the bellhop a five right off the bat. Remember that bellhop has your bags.

Check-in is a breeze; Gold Club Service has its advantages. They don't know it yet but I don't roll like that anymore. Well to make it look good, I'll still play the roll. First we need to get settled.

We get a two-bedroom suite at a very good casino rate, free. The room is really nothing to brag about but it is very functional. The suite has two bedrooms, two baths, a nice size sitting area, and a large screen TV.

The bags arrive and I set out some things to get comfortable in. I chose a beige fitted tee shirt to go with a loose fitting pair of emerald green golf shorts by Nike. My Kenneth Cole sandals finish off the look. Even with my casual dress I still wear my Raymond Weil watch and rings so that at one glance it's clear that one should not be fooled by the casual style of dress.

Well, it's time to take on Vegas again.

Chapter 3
Vegas Strategy

When I go to Vegas, the first thing I do is get to know the casino host at the hotel where I am staying. My strategy is to establish a line of credit. About fifteen thousand dollars will do the trick. Just go down and give the host a few credit card numbers and you will have it.

Don't take it the wrong way, I'm not in any way suggesting that I am actually going to gamble with fifteen thousand dollars, but the fact that the casino knows that I could if I wanted to buys me a little something. It's just a start but it is a good start. Now you know the casino host on a first name basis and he knows that you have at least fifteen thousand dollars that you can spend in his casino. The complimentary items that you want are a little closer.

Casinos pass out complimentary rooms, show tickets, food, airplane travel, etc., based upon your perceived play. It does not pay to spread yourself too thin. Action at one casino is enough. The next thing is to keep reminding yourself that gambling never pays. The casino is using every trick in the book to part you from your money. When gambling, your emotions are your worst enemy. You can never have control of all of your emotions. The best thing for you to do is to not start gambling. No one can tell what effect a first hit of a drug or alcohol will have on a person. Just like drugs or alcohol can do, gambling can start you down a hill that leads to ruin. Take it from me, I know first hand.

* * *

I remember how it all began. It was during my first Christmas with Charity. I gave her a seven-day vacation cruise to the Bahamas. It was a really good present for the both of us. She agreed to go and it forced me to get some R&R that I may have passed up under normal circumstances. We flew from Chicago to Miami to catch the cruise. It was coach of course. Using my connections with the opposite sex could turn out to be embarrassing.

All flight attendants have the ability to fly at will, at little or no cost. If a flight attendant wanted to be where you were flying to on vacation, they could with little or no effort. As such, the situation called for the use of a different airline, so my flight plans wouldn't be pulled up on the computers that my regular attendants have access to. It also mandated that I keep my mouth closed about where I was going. That meant to everyone, unless it was absolutely necessary.

In this situation, I had to keep people on a need-to-know basis. With there only being six degrees of separation, one never knows who might inadvertently drop a dime on you. Those closest to you are the ones that can hurt you; and generally it happens in the most innocent of ways. Keep your mouth shut or don't blame anyone besides yourself for the consequences.

Our trip was for seven days, four islands, and not a care in the world. We do all of the normal things that cruise goers do. There is bingo, island hopping, sex, drinking, more sex, all coupled with a little exercise in the ship's gym; you know the drill. What I was not prepared for was the casino that was onboard the ship. Boy that casino called me into her by flashing her shining lights and ringing her bells of fortune. Never having the desire to gamble before, I was ill equipped to handle the fast paced games of chance.

I took my first chance at Blackjack, a game that I grew up playing at home. How hard could it be? Having no idea of the rules of the game or proper player table manners, I soon made enemies of all the players at the table while losing one hundred dollars in about fifteen minutes. Disheartened by the Blackjack table, I went over to the Roulette table and bought in for another hundred dollars.

Each spin of the wheel brought more money, until I was a two-hundred dollar winner. Cashing in, I could not wait to tell Charity about my winnings. It was a defining moment in my life. If there were a way to predict how the winning of this small sum of money would change me, I would have checked into gamblers anonymous right then and there.

Over the next five days, I visited my new past-time every evening; never breaking even, and in most cases depositing a couple hundred dollars for my efforts. The games, Blackjack, Roulette, Caribbean Stud Poker, and the slot machines seemed so easy. However, the results were all the same - I lost money. If that was not enough, my nightly visits to the casino were cutting into the time that I spent with Charity - an issue that caused the first real disagreement in our nine-month-old, hot as fire, relationship.

By the seventh night, my losses were over one thousand dollars and I was happy to spend the evening with Charity. She was happy because the itch to gamble was out of my system. I was still boiling on the inside and what had always been a strength for me began to become a liability. Always rising to a challenge, I began wondering if there was a way to win at these games.

The vacation was fun and even with my extensive gaming activities I was able to catch enough sun that people asked where I had been. Keeping with my need to know attitude, I just replied that I was playing in a softball tournament and had caught some extra sun.

It wasn't too long after our vacation, while walking hand in hand down Oak Street on the near north side of Chicago, Charity and I passed a Super Crown bookstore on our way to see a movie. When we got to the box office, we found out the movie that we wanted to see was sold out. It would be forty-five minutes before the next showing of the movie. We bought tickets to the next showing of the movie and decided to walk back to the bookstore to waste a little time.

Charity loves books and bookstores. I have seen her spend hours on end in them. After entering the store, she quickly disappeared into the stacks of books. I inquire to one of the sales people if the store has books on card games? I am directed to a section in the store that has three bookcases full of books on gambling.

I spent thirty minutes selecting eleven books on gambling. In the movie, I could hardly concentrate wanting to get to pages of the books and the hidden secrets therein.

Over the next two weeks, I studied the books like a professor doing research to find a cure for AIDS. Not one of the references gave the practical advice of don't gamble. Each one of them definitively stated that you could beat the odds and win. Of course, it did cross my mind if they were such good gamblers, why were they writing books and not gambling. Most of the authors of the books gave an explanation that they were so good that they had been barred from the casinos.

With the research being done it had not crossed my mind to find a casino to test it in. At that time the research was still being viewed by me as an "if I am ever in that situation again" type of informational resource tool. Then it happened. I had begun to concentrate on the game of Blackjack as one that was foolproof.

The strategies that were presented in the books seemed sound. The rules did not vary and all of the expert advice that was given in the book said you would win if you follow the rules.

On a trip to Hawaii, Charity and I had an overnight layover in Las Vegas. It was perfect, I could test my newly acquired knowledge at a real casino and it would not cost me anything to do it.

Charity and I got off the plane and placed our bags in a locker. The dry heat took our breath away as soon as the doors to the airport terminal were behind us. It was 11:00 p.m. and the heat was still stifling. We found a cab and asked the driver where the best place was to go and see some of Las Vegas. Of course his reply was the Strip.

Being acquainted with the MGM Grand Hotel by its outline from the plane's window when we were landing, I directed the driver to take us there. We walked around for a while. We visited the lobby of the MGM. When we walked outside we were overwhelmed by vendor after vendor selling tee shirts or handing out flyers about exotic women able to do exotic things for a "price." Needing relief from the parching heat, we went into the Tropicana Hotel and looked around. It was nothing special and it did not hold our attention for very long.

Across the street was the Excalibur Hotel. While walking into the front door of the hotel, we were treated to a display of knights in armor acting out the days of King Arthur. Once inside, the decor was enough to make you want to stay awhile. It was about one o'clock a.m. Las Vegas time when Charity decided to go exploring the hotel on her own, so I settled in at a five-dollar Blackjack table.

Having memorized the rules for playing the game, I bought into the game for one hundred dollars. For the next four hours, I played by the rules that the books had taught and never added to my ten dollar bet. When all is said and done, I cashed in for two hundred sixty-one dollars - I was on cloud nine.

I find Charity at a nickel slot machine. We cash in Charity's nickels and have just enough time to catch a cab back to the airport and make our flight to Hawaii. Feeling like I had found a genie in a bottle, I can't wait until the next time to play.

Over the next year, I graduate from blackjack, to craps, and onto one of the most unforgettable losing streaks that anyone could ever imagine. The more I lost, the more I played. The more I played, the farther away from Charity I drove myself. The further away that I went, the more my business, real estate holdings, bank account, and my awareness of how far I had fallen, plunged. It wasn't long before I was on the brink of bankruptcy owing money to everyone including Charity.

In a state of depression, death seemed like a good way out. On the brink of suicide, I locked myself in my loft condominium apartment with the desire and means to end it all. For the next three months the tailspin, that currently was my life, kept spiraling downward.

Fortunately, I was shielded from it all since I divorced myself from everyone in the world except Charity. She was great. To this day she does not know that she is the reason that I am alive. My letting her down by having her find my decaying body was too much to set on anyone. Moreover, while I was in hell and giving her the blues, she kept right on giving me her everything.

During the first two months of my seclusion, I lost contact with everything including myself. I spent countless hours in PJs looking into deep space. At least for me it was deep space. Everyone else knew that it was just my living-room.

Charity defended me from all outside influences. She had my home phone calls forwarded to her office. She informed all of my creditors that I was ill and would take care of bills when I was better. Friends and business associates were informed that I was out of the country.

After being locked away for two months, Charity attempted a different approach to reach me. Having grown tired of my self-pity, she gave me an ultimatum - shit or get off the pot.

Charity set up an appointment with a therapist for my problems; my going to see him was not up for debate. I had not been out of the house in two months; a fact that my grooming revealed. Charity took the next two weeks off work to be there for me.

The counseling sessions were very emotional and revealed things that had been long forgotten by me. Somehow, with the grace of God, I made it back. However, the trip back didn't end before I lost every thing- including Charity. The bad part is that through it all, and true to my form, to this day, I have never said thank you to Charity.

Chapter 4
Daryl Shows His Colors

"Charity, it's Daryl ... I told you I would call you with the 4-1-1. Dee hasn't said what this is all about but I'm certain that he is planning something stupid that will be a big mistake; you know he's so impulsive ... Girl, I've known Dee for a long time and let me tell you he has never been happier than when he was with you ... You know he still loves you ... Let me get off this phone, girl, the roaming charges are going to kill me. You're still coming aren't you? ... Good girl. We're at the Flamingo ... Don't forget, let me set up the meeting between you two ... I'll be there so you don't have nothing to worry about. I've got this one covered ... See you early Thursday at the airport. Lov ya, bye."

That boy better be thankful for what I'm doing for him. Ever since I met Dee he has been pulling strange shit like this. Like we don't know what people do in Vegas - with no waiting period and a wedding taking place twenty-four seven - it's a perfect place to get married. Lisa doesn't get here until Friday morning. Charity will be here Thursday. That gives us one day to work some magic. If I play my cards right, Dee and Charity will be married before Lisa arrives, sorry Lisa but they belong together. Well, we only live once so I've got to get this right the first time. Darryl spoke out loud to himself.

Chapter 5
Charity Confesses

I love Dee. That says a lot after everything he put me through. Just to hear his voice does something to me. I guess when you're dealing with someone as intense as he is the highs are very high and boy are the lows low. I just don't want things to end without me at least telling him that he is in my heart - for that matter, under my skin, in my bones, in my very being. How did things get so bad that we had to break up and stay broken? I just wanted him to hurt like he was hurting me and tearing my dreams from me.

When I met Dee, I was a young girl without direction. Somehow he saw me. He was bold with all the answers and I fell for him. It's hard to explain what happens when you find your soul mate. When two people are meant for each other, all rhyme and reason goes out of the window and things just happen naturally. All of the games to keep men guessing, that women learn to play as girls and continue to play into womanhood, are waylaid out of the window. You just fall hard. Honestly, I could not stay away from him. We made mad love constantly; in the car, on the floor, in every room of the house.

We would share long sexy baths that included sex, caressing each other, sex, washing each other, and more sex. Our bath was followed by us being wrapped in each other's arms sleeping the night away. If I was lucky, I would wake in the morning to his tongue sending vibes of passion from my middle straight up to my brain. How does a man learn how to do that? He was the first to show what making love could be like when you put your partner's wants and needs first.

Dee taught me to slow down and enjoy each other. He would say, "Slow down, Charity, it's not going anywhere."

Sundays were our special time together. Many times our lovemaking would last through lunch and dinner. We would start out on a Sunday afternoon wrapped in a blanket on the family room floor watching an old black and white movie on television.

Dee has a way of paying attention to the least sexiest part of my body and making it sexy. Once during a back rub he licked every inch of my back and neck. Not wet and sloppy but soft and slow. Drying each inch with cool breaths before proceeding to the next inch of me. My body shook under his care. He must have spent an hour doing this. I really don't know how long because partway through it, I was so relaxed that I fell into a deep slumber, only to be awakened by soft cheek kisses designed to bring me out of my restful state slowly, and building to amorousness.

Those days also included truthful conversations about our wants and desires. There were discussions about our schedules for the upcoming week including us carving out time to spend together. Dee would try to act interested while I caught up on a week's worth of videotaped stories - All My Children, One Life To Live, and General Hospital. It was during these times that Dee would solve any problems that might have occurred during the week. He would do it for our extended family and me.

Just give him a set of facts and he will give you a solution that's not only unique but that also works. His knack of getting to the bottom of a person's motivations is uncanny. He is responsible for much of my rise in sales. All the while we would play board games which would be followed by our cooking dinner for each other. The night is finished with wine and a bath.

Spoiled and not realizing that all men are not mentally, physically, or emotionally equivalent, I let our relationship collapse. The collapse was because I had lost all faith in him. For upwards of three months, I had given my all to helping him with his issues, especially gambling. Dee was in a depressed state over mounting gambling debts. I'm sure at that time someone named Quido was looking for him near the Chicago River. At any rate, I did everything I could to help. The last straw was when I found out that he had been back to the casino. I lost it right then and there. Money that I had given him to help sort things out had gone to gambling again. I couldn't believe it. I thought he was cured through counseling; boy was I wrong.

Out of options and too outdone, I detached him from my life and briefly from my thoughts. After Dee I found myself comparing each potential suitor with him. My current actions speak on how they faired.

I know that going to Las Vegas to confront Dee may not be the best plan in the world. What other options do I have other then giving up? Dee and I stopped talking just after the break-up. He said it hurt too much. For the last two weeks, he has not returned any of my calls. So, at this point, my options are limited considering what I've got to work with.

Chapter 6
Dee Talks About His Boy Len

I finished my work with Dave Wilson, the casino host. I got three player's cards in my name and went back to the room to educate the boys on how to earn complimentary things from the hotel.

Back in the room, everybody was laid out recovering from their first exposure to the dry Vegas heat. Len was up watching the tube. One of those continuously running programs that purport to teach you how to play the casino games. What they in fact do, is make you comfortable enough to cozy up to a gaming table and part with some cash. Len hasn't changed since college; he's still looking for the angles.

I met Len the second week into my freshman year at Northern Illinois University. We were both headed into the unknown; we were about to join the Alpha's spring pledge line. Len was flamboyant. All of the pretty little fraternity sisters that we called angels took care of his every situation while we were on line.

Three people started on my pledge line including myself. Len and I stuck out the twelve weeks and went over the burning sands into Alpha land. Being the new kids on the block, we exploded. Over the next three and a half years while we were in school, we were inseparable.

The big brothers decided to nickname Len BOP. Tall and lanky with weathered deep lemony skin that showed a little age, he was clearly their spec which actually meant the big brothers preferred him over me hence the name spec meaning special. Unaffected by time was Len's broad, full smile that also brightened his eyes and routinely stopped traffic. His role was typecast for him right from the start. Artsy by nature, Len majored in Visual Communication.

One walk into his dorm room and his artsy nature and desire to have as many women as possible was made clear. He had a single room on the tenth floor of Stevenson Towers South. In his two hundred square foot room, there was a loft bed complete with black satin sheets, a phone with answering machine and caller identification, wall to wall carpeting, a slide projector, and enough artwork to start a small museum, surely not the average college dorm room. Len's place reminded me more of a thirty-five year old man's bachelor pad.

The tales that the women told after being alone in Len's room implored the curiosity of many a woman to suggest that they should be the next one to experience the flavor of the room or shall I say the flavor of Len himself. It was amazing how the room worked a party. Len would just tell a woman to meet him at his room after the party and slip her his spare room key. After the party, she would be there waiting to become a part of history. He was that kind of guy. He barely had to open his mouth and woman came running.

The relationship between Len and me was unique from the start. The norm is that male friends will spend hours together and never exchange the least bit of useful information. They talk day and night about sports, who shot John, etc., but never have a conversation that provides value. Len and I were both secure within our abilities and did not see each other as a threat. This rarity between men allowed us to help each other become better men. Len having my back helped me get through school and provided a close friend to talk to when there was no one else.

As simple as it sounds, without that type of support, many men never achieve their potential in life. Len was my ace all through school. It also didn't hurt that we could exchange stories on the women we were dealing with or what women we wanted to deal with. To this day, I know that he would lay down his life for me and I would do the same for him. If I've got it, he can have it. If he says the sky is purple, then the sky is purple. No questions asked.

Seeing Len pay attention to the television, while they were explaining the rules of playing the gambling games, caused me concern since we are so similar. Getting the gambling bug out of Len's ear would be easy. It is just a simple matter of substitution. Len loves women as much as I do. With little effort, I set the night's agenda with BOP. We would spend the night at the clubs meeting as many women as possible. Len, having the best skills between all of us, was eager to use those skills to ensure that we had the best time that we could have.

We rested until about seven p.m., then got dressed for the evening. While getting dressed, I ordered room service and charged it to the room. After getting dressed and eating, we left the room, went to the lobby, and had the doorman hail us a cab. We took the cab to Club Rio. We walked in the club at about 9:15 p.m. the club was just getting started. Before I knew it, two professional hookers joined us at the bar. It was clear from the way that Al and Daryl were pushing up on them that they had no idea the girls were working. In time, I was able to secretly whisper to the girls my intentions. I gave each of the two girls - Heather and Beth - a fifty dollar bill and whispered, "Be nice! There's more where that came from." It was clear from the conversation, that Daryl was deceived by the girl's looks to the point of not having a clue that they were professionals.

Len pulled Al's coat and we proceeded to make this a night that Daryl would never forget. Len pulled Beth away from the party and set the deal; both girls in the room with Daryl having his pick of the two. Len made it clear to the girls and us, that Daryl was to think that it was his conversation that got them both back to the room. With the deed done, Len and I settled in to watch things develop.

About twenty minutes later, Daryl was clearly, in his mind, in control of the situation. Hedging his bets, he firmly asked both Heather and Beth, "Why don't we take the party back to my suite?"

Playing their part, they replied, "Sure, is everybody going?"

"That's up to you guys but I think I've got this one covered."

* * *

Knowing the nature of Vegas women, we couldn't let Daryl go off by himself and maybe get taken. I left Al with Len and took a fast cab back to the room. My cab must have been fast, or the driver of Daryl's cab must be getting an eyeful and driving real slow so as not to miss any action. I keyed the door and proceeded to move all of our things to the main bedroom. I locked the door from inside the room just before I heard the suite door open.

I proceeded to turn on the television and lay back on the bed. A member of the hotel's staff had turned back the bed and placed an after dinner mint on the bed pillow along with some papers. They all went to the floor under the light of the television. The television was making shadows on the wall that took my tired mind to a semi-conscience state - bordering between sleep and awake. There I started thinking back to when I was young on my grandfather's farm.

Chapter 7
Dee's Past With His Grandfather

Every summer, until I was fourteen, was spent on my grandfather's farm outside of McAllister, Oklahoma. The appreciation of the farm is not something that you are born with; it is something that is developed over the years. Grandfather Miller Carter was the type of man that made you have appreciation fast - a firm appreciation of how good it felt when the work stopped that is. It's like the man who is banging his head against the wall. When he stops, it is as if his life has been given back to him.

Work on a farm is never ending. It is essential to your peace of mind that, from time to time, you stop and take an inventory of what has been accomplished thus far. If one was to not look at the present accomplishments and only look at the never ending tasks ahead, he begins to hate the farm life.

Out in the backwoods exists a life that has been all but forgotten. A life where in the spring time you pick out the calf that will mature and provide for the family's needs in the fall and winter. A life where spring brings planting that develops into cash producing crops.

The following spring brings a reinvestment of the cash in seed, animals, and equipment that starts the cycle all over again. For those that are making progress, farming is an acceptable lifestyle. For those that are going backwards because of a bad harvest, sick animals, not enough rain, etc., farming is a backbreaking job that has no end.

Having had his share of bad years on the farm, these days that allow us to sit back, watch the crops rise to the nurturing sun and the calf to fatten, are cherished. With the farm being modernized and most of the land leased out to bigger operations, cultivating his family was now Miller's biggest task in life. This task was like child's play when his grandchildren are at the farm. The measure of a man's life is not only what he did while he was here on this earth, but also what he leaves behind to grow.

In Miller's life, he wanted to leave some knowledge with his grandchildren that would allow the Carter name to mean something in the years to come. Miller tried hard to have the same emotional attachment with each of the six grandchildren that he had been blessed with. However, his natural grandchild was me and not my cousins; I had to be his favorite. The other grandchildren each represented a break in the Carter bloodline. Miller's oldest son, Miller Jr., adopted his three children when the doctors told him and his wife Betty that they would never conceive children of their own.

Miller's stepdaughter Libby has two adorable children. When the children came to the farm, Miller showed them all of the love that could be expected from a grandparent. His wife, having died years earlier, had never seen the farm as a successful enterprise. She had only seen the despair of the early years when it seemed that they would have to abandon the farm altogether.

The farm was home to an extended family. There was Cousin Snukum who looked every day of one hundred ten years old, Miller's sister Pearl, and a host of relations always coming by to visit or stay a few days. There was always enough love on the farm to and from everyone.

Miller's youngest son Frank had his wife Zephyr living on the farm when his last grandchild was born. I'm that last grandchild. I was born on a bright sunny July day. I was told that the heat in the house while I was being born was overbearing. Through the heat, after fourteen hours of labor, in a small bedroom set off from the kitchen, in a home that was little more than a shack came me.

A natural bond was forged from the start between grandfather and grandson. It was as if my being born into the old house brought a new air of hope. Hope turned into determination. Determination guided the household through the turbulent sixties to the newfound prosperity of the seventies. No, I didn't do anything overtly spectacular. However, my birth in my grandfather's house brought change almost instantly.

My Grandfather, a proud man, worked hard his entire life. The coal mines of the deep southwest were his school ground. At five-foot-nine inches tall, two hundred sixty-five pounds, no fat to speak of, he was a barrel of a man and his physical strength was evident. Most who knew him respected him, and where he could not command respect, his physical presence stood in its place. There were many who were bigger and stronger, but none that had all three tools; physical size, respect of his race, and the gift of being able to talk and write the king's English in such a way that could persuade the most racist white man to at least consider his words. For over thirty years, he was the leader of the Negro contingent of workers in the coal mines throughout Oklahoma and Alabama.

Through cave-ins, floods, worker strikes, and death, before the days of OSHA, my grandfather led the way keeping the black workers a strong unified force. Thirty years and a case of black lung disease later, it was time for him to retire from the mine. At age fifty-one it was too early to retire and do nothing, so the farm came into being. Heavy rains, drought, pests, you name it, it hit the farm. It made grandfather one of the few farmers of his day that paid hard earned cash for the right to farm the land.

Since my birth, the farm experienced fortune that was unbeknownst before now. Out of the blue, the corn grew, cows had calves, eggs hatched. As a result of the new found fortune, there was plenty to sell; and sell the Carters did. All was good and it showed in the improvements around the farm. When grandfather's age started to catch up with him, he was able to lease portions of the farm's two hundred acres to the larger concerns that were taking over farming in the area. With the diminished workload of the farm, there was more time to spend with grandchildren. This quality time made his life well worth living. It was during this time that grandfather taught me everything he could in as little time as possible.

* * *

Grandfather had a habit of telling stories of his life and the lives of those that came before him. Of all the history that I have ever learned or that has been told to me - years of history learned from uninformed teachers in different schools that had the sole goal of you mastering "his story" as outlined in the pages of a four inch text book - bore none of the passion of the past people that accompanied the everyday life of those making the history. Years of history depicted by the despair in many of the black communities of today.

There are years of history that have edited out the past triumphs of an entire people. No, granddaddy's history lessons were from the recollection of one born in eighteen hundred ninety- seven. First generation removed from slavery. His father, age sixty-one at the time of

Miller's birth, married a full blooded American Indian.

Granddaddy's physical appearance corroborated an ancestral history that included being bred for physical strength. An accidental by-product was the breeding for strength of character. Clearly, the slave master would mate together the brightest, hardest working slaves that also had the physical qualities of a bull.

Granddaddy only stood about 5'-9" tall. The red skin tone that was a gift from his mother was evident. Black straight hair and slanted coal black eyes that could read your mind. One glance told you that this was a serious man and was not to be toyed with in any fashion. It was this same man that provided the only time in my life that everything revolved around me. Even when my other cousins were around, I was still aware that my needs and many times my wants came first. It's a special relationship that grandchildren need to have with their grandparents; a relationship that if you missed it as a child you will most likely never know. It's a feeling of having the world revolve around you. If you're lucky enough to experience it, you will try, sometimes in vain, to get back to it.

Grandfather sure could tell a story. When he spoke, his words were full of character. His voice transcended time and allowed a listener to be transported back ten, twenty, thirty ... as many years as it takes. His voice filled my brain with a stream of knowledge that, used correctly, navigates me through the roads of today. These were roads full of potholes of racial hatred, envy, self pity, and despair; potholes that would knock many a good man off his stride, never to regain full form or get back on track in the direction of his rightful place.

Throughout my years, I learned more from the recounting of granddaddy's memories about people in general- their motivations, strengths, weaknesses, and character - than from any other source - be it book, human or otherwise. No other medium was as clear, as lucid, as informed, as impassioned. Human nature was rationalized to the point that cause and effect was made clear to a young man still finding his way.

The first story that I remember granddaddy telling me was when I was about seven. The last story was when I was twenty-two, just before he quietly faded away from our lives; years of stories that when told to me many times did not click or were too advance for my young mind. You can bet that those very stories to this day guide me through many an untenable situation.

Think about this very simple question; who are you? Many times when I have to pick myself off the ground I think of one of my grandfather's story, and find the answer to this very question.

On a hazy fall day, the sun was going down. Out of the blue, as usual, granddaddy asked a question. "Dee, who are you? Where in the hell did you come from?"

Giving his question some thought, as I had been trained to do, I came up with the answer of a thirteen-year-old child. Slowly, carefully, with aforethought I responded,

"Granddaddy, I am De Acquinn Carter. I was born over there in that house," I began my reply to his question while pointing a proud finger at the home that started out as an abandoned shack and over the years has been refurbished with room additions - three - and modern conveniences - indoor plumbing, electricity, and appliances. Through all of the changes, the home has retained its charm and harmony with the land. "My Dad's name is...," I tried to continue only to be cut off with the beginning of a story that I had never heard before.

Imagine Dee, that you were locked in a place about the size of that barn over there with about one thousand other people. Chained lying down on hard wooden cots stacked one on top of each other; stacked twenty high. You're given just enough food - hard bread - and water to keep you alive. You eat and drink every seven or eight days during the time that you're unchained from your cot for your twenty minutes on the deck out of the dark dank confines of the ship's bowels. While chained to the cot, the guy chained to the cot above you defecated and urinated on you since there was no other place for him to go. With gravity taking its course, the excretions fell onto the woman below you and then oozed onto the person below her. The mess would travel on from there until it rested either on the people or on the bottom of the hold. Either way, in about two weeks, the whole place smelled of death.

Maggots found food in the defecation as well as in the dead human bodies and live people who happen to have open wounds or defecation sitting on them. With no way to wipe the mess off of you, two months into the voyage, a third - about four hundred - of your mates are dead. You are given the chore of discarding the dead's bodies. The bodies are thrown over the side of the boat to waiting sharks.

Sharks also are an effective deterrent to you jumping overboard to try and swim back home. After three months, thousands of miles away from home, only four hundred of your mates are left. When you are let off the boat you are sold into slavery. The four hundred slaves that got the privilege to be sold into slavery were the physically strong and mentally tough. One without the other was not good enough to warrant survival during the journey. Those that lived were tough enough not to will themselves to die throughout the ordeal. Having the mental capacity and the physical strength to survive, when death was the easiest path to take.

Dee, you are a descendant of the best of the best that the great continent of Africa had to offer. The product of an unnatural selection process that weeded out those who could dilute us from being the best. A process that continued for over four hundred years through a mating process that bred us for the best qualities of temperament and physical strength. Qualities that were only tainted by the raping of the black woman by people not worthy to plant a seed.

The story and its implications were not fully understood by me until much later in my life. My response to my granddaddy was, "Why do you have to tell me such horrible stories?"

I can remember many of the changes that happened to the farm over the years. From summer to summer, the farm went from an outhouse and well water to indoor plumbing. From a home that had no conveniences to one that had every modern convenience of the day.

The family, in a relatively short period of time, became the envy of the county. Boy, did they cook in that house or what? The kitchen always smelled of homemade biscuits, home smoked ham, chitterlings, country fried steak, mustard and collard greens, cabbage, cornbread, sweet potatoes, all kinds of good things to eat. All of the smells were meshed inside the very fiber of the house. When you walked into the house the smells that overcame you, even when there was nothing cooking, made this house home.

The house and all of the people are all gone now. I wonder if they knew that they had such an impact on me. They had to know, didn't they?

Chapter 8
Charity and Her Mom

Meeting Charity's mother Ms. Johnson was a trip. On a lazy Sunday afternoon, Charity and I settled into my car and headed down Dearborn Street over to the I- 290 Expressway. It was about a twenty-minute ride to Maywood for most drivers. I drive sometimes two or three hundred miles a day so I have a habit of keeping my foot in it. For me it's an enjoyable fifteen-minute drive. I get off the expressway at the 9th Street exit and hang a left onto 9th. Charity's mom's house is about four blocks down.

It's hard to believe that a neighborhood can change so fast. Charity's mother's house looks out of place with its freshly painted trim, new replacement windows, carefully trimmed grass, and well manicured bushes. Her house is contrasted by frame and brick bungalows that are in need of repair. The homes are victimized by white flight coupled with replacement families that stretched their budgets just to buy a house. With no money in the budget for home repairs, the effects of neglect quickly begin to show on the homes that are in the latter stages of their useful life.

Parked in front, Charity and I went into the house. Once inside of the house, Charity called for her mama to come meet us in the front room. The smell of the Sunday dinner cooking was enough to take me right from the Midwest and into the Deep South on a Sunday summer's day in Mc Alister, Oklahoma.

Charity hugged her mother when she came up from the back of the house. Her mother's hug took all of Charity's vibrancy from her. It was as if right before your eyes Ms. Johnson took and Charity gave her very being. All of that giving seemed like it added ten years to Charity's age. Her mother greedily accepted all that was offered and took a little extra, too.

Charmaine Johnson was a piece of work. Her look was that of someone who was trying to hold on to her youth. Surely, with a twenty-six year old daughter, this woman was at least in her forties. Her style and mannerisms were of one much younger. She lived for and garnered most of her strength from her daughter. From the start, it was clear that she viewed me with the contempt that one would have for a burglar that came over to her house to case it - case it to steal her most valuable possession. It showed through the facade of a smile with witch she greeted me in her living room.

She was built small - about five-feet-one-inch and one hundred five pounds. Her size aside, this was a very sturdy woman. Her will was imparted onto everything that came into her path. Strikingly pretty with an oval face and skin the color of a fall pecan. In direct sunlight or well placed indoor light, a hint of deep red color highlighted from her face.

Her hair, sandy in color, flowed down her back with a flip that covered one eye. Her hair style - meant for a younger woman - made you want to reach out and brush her thick bang back from her eyes to show the full beauty of her face.

Just minutes before when she came into the room, this woman had all the life of a ninety year old woman. Now after coming into contact with her daughter, she became reborn and radiant. She was so striking that the color in her peach pants suit seemed to come alive also.

Her mother spoke slowly, like a woman twice her age. Her southern accent was clear when she attacked. "So you're here to get my blessings for you to take my daughter from me," she said with no emotion in her voice or on her face. "Well, you're not going to get it," she said with a smirk that made it unclear if she was serious or joking. "My baby is all I have left," she said with a fire in her eyes that made me look down to the floor. "If you take her, that will be the end of me."

Having no idea where this was coming from or where it was going, I tried to give myself some time to get my bearings by just saying

"Excuse me" and continuing to divert my eyes to the floor. Gaining my bearings, I simply said to this woman, "You have me all wrong. I just want to be a part of things. Charity told me that you guys are close and I would never dream of coming between you two." My eyes now fully engaging hers with a daring look that told her, in unspoken words, that this line of dialog was over. This exchange was just the beginning of a triangle that would tear at the fiber of Charity's peace for years.

After the exchange of looks between Ms. Johnson and me, there was a cool in the room that iced everyone in their tracks. I broke the ice with a comment about the smell coming from the back of the house. "Ms. Johnson are those homemade biscuits that I smell back there," I said it with a smile that had to be three feet wide. It was greeted with a return smile that said, “Boy are you still here?" followed by a crisp "Yes it is!"

"Well, maybe next time I come I can sample some of them. I just came by with Charity and I have a few more stops to make. Charity can you walk me to the door?"

The look on Charity's face spelled volumes, she had no idea what just happened and the color was just returning to her face. "Don't worry baby, she just has to get used to you having someone special in your life besides her. She will come around." I didn't believe it but I knew that I had to get out of there before things got worse. I asked Charity to call me later and ran out the front door to my car, not even thinking about what just happened.

* * *

"Mama! What was that all about?"

Charmaine contorted her face like a prune and in one breath expelled, "That man ain't right for you girl. Believe you me, he ain't and I won't have anything to do with it. Time will tell- you listen to your old Mama. I don't ask for much; just bring home a man who will be right – right for you – right for us. That man you brought in here cares only about himself. Just look at him and you can tell that he thinks that he is better than we are. I tell you girl, that's a man who will hurt you."

"Mama you can't pick and choose who I go out with. Besides, you don't even know Dee. I can't believe that you just reared back and took his head off."

"Listen girl, you don't get to be fifty-five years old without learning a little something about people. That boy that you brought in here is just like ... Why am I explaining myself? I don't "

"Just like what Mama?" Charity cut her mother off in mid sentence. Now Charity started to dig in for a fight. "Like the daddy that I've never known? How could you possibly know that after seeing him for all of two seconds before you crucified him and embarrassed the hell out of me?"

"Don't forget yourself girl, I'm still the mama here."

"I can't know who my father is! Nobody that I bring home is good enough! What do you want from me?" With that being said the tears started to fall. Not just tears for the day but tears of built-up frustration at having half of your heritage as an enigma to you without knowing why.

Chapter 9
Charity's Mom Tells it Like It Is

That girl still thinks that life is like "Leave It to Beaver" and after thirty minutes all of the world's issues are solved. Well life isn't and she'd better get over it. That boy she brought over here gives me the creeps. His face makes me think of the past. Back when I was thirty-one years old and still as fresh as the day I was born. Saving myself for the right time, the right place, and the right person – my husband.

At thirty-one and unmarried, in those times, you are considered spinster material and you begin to have self doubts and start to wonder what you are doing wrong. Yea I wondered what was wrong with me. I looked in the mirror and at first glance decided that it was not my looks that were an issue. Always the first to have a date for the weekend and the last to have a second date, let alone a steady boyfriend.

I was working the checkout as a civilian worker in the base's PX – Post Exchange – at Great Lakes Naval Base. Here he comes, with his fine brazen ass, with the nerve to ask me to dinner right there while standing in my checkout line. Like I said, I was wondering. I mean not being formally introduced and all - I was wondering. Him being a little too old for my taste - at least five or more years older than me - I'm wondering. All of my wondering was complete in about two seconds and I replied, "Sailor, if you're just looking for a good time, there are other girls on this base."

"No sister, you've got me all wrong. I asked you to go to dinner with me. I don't need you to show me a good time. What kind of food you like anyway? Maybe I can't afford a pretty woman like you."

It's funny how it's usually something very remote that will entice you to let your guard down. It was not the Viet Nam battle-earned medals on his chest. Nor was it the three stripes on his arms that showed that he could afford a family and me if he wanted to. It was his teeth, strong, white, crisp, and clean; the perfect complement to that white uniform that was draped over those muscles. Me with my well earned lower plate, I was in love with perfect teeth. He had them.

With the real wondering just getting started, I said yes to his southern charm. I said yes to those teeth. Not knowing myself in that way, without my knowledge, my insides said yes to everything. After dinner, we went for a walk down the shores of Lake Michigan. My wondering, coupled with his experienced ways, took my mind to places that I was always taught not to go.

As you know, the mind is the first thing to go. I must have lost mine. Many have tried in the past to handle my jewels but each one was met with a firm, "I'm saving that for my husband." This time when he reached out to touch me, I was not as firm. I calmly informed him, "I am saving that."

It was met with a confident, "Okay honey, I've got something to save too. He lightly brushed both of his thumbs against my aroused nipples. The left one reacted with an uncontrollable reaction that went straight to my brain. Don't ask me why I let him continue; I just don't know. Like I said, the mind is the first thing to go - go it did. My body was exploding like a school girl on her prom opening up to the world for the first time.

Everything I had read, everyone I had talked to in the past said that the first time would hurt like hell. My mama hadn't prepared me for anything. I was taken aback when he felt so fine. He felt finer than he looked and no one could have told me that I was not a complete woman. With books and movies showing everything nowadays, I know that my doctor was right that I am technically still a virgin.

For eleven nights he came to me. Hungry for knowledge, I explored every inch of his body. Today, if I tried, I could remember every hair on his tight ass, the mole on his balls. I can remember his circumcised manhood and the one eye that appeared and disappeared in my hand as I caressed him repeatedly. Eleven nights of being wrapped in his arms; ten sunrises with his body entwined with mine so tightly that my heart took his heart's rhythm.

A blessing occurred somewhere between sundown and sunrise on one of the eleven nights. A seed found its ways inside of me with the bumping and grinding, caressing and feeling, and me not knowing. Together we did everything, except the final act. Me not knowing he was respecting his family and my wish to wait until I had a husband.

Through it all, there was one rub too many. Day twelve he was gone. Three months before I had a clue. Five months before my first prenatal care. Seven months before I tracked him down. Eight months before he came clean about his family. Nine months when I listed a black boy, killed in action, on the birth certificate as the child's father. Two days to name my child Charity. It was the charity of God that brought her to me when there was nothing else to cling to.

The doctor could not believe that I was in a virginal state with me being five months into my pregnancy. With a C-section, Charity came into my life. With her, the loss of my family seemed worth it. As soon as my mama found out that I was with child, she soundly informed me not to come back to Columbus, Mississippi without a husband. I have not been back since. Likewise, no other man has touched me since.

How can I explain to Charity that this boy's essence is so similar to her dad's? He was trouble and I know that this boy will be trouble too. She wants me to just sit back and let her do this. I would be less than a mother not to let her know what my insides tell me about this boy.

Chapter 10
Dee's Next Morning in Vegas; Where's My Boy?

It's four in the morning and the television is ringing in my ear. Feeling like I'm dreaming and the sound of the TV is part of the dream, it takes a few minutes for me to figure out where I am and what the aggravating sound is that's ringing in my ear. Gaining my senses, I stumble out of the bed and hit the on/off button on the TV. Sitting back on the bed, it starts to come back to me when I realize that I was supposed to be looking out for Daryl. Sleep on the job-who would have guessed that I would be sleep on the job.

It's times like this that I hate sleeping alone. Once you get used to having a warm body next to you every night, sleeping alone just doesn't cut it. Don't get me wrong, waking up with the wrong person is worst then having no one there at all. The right person, one that your body can curl up to and share each other's warmth until you are fully awake, is like sleeping with a little piece of heaven. Waking up this way has been known to erase morning headaches as well as other minor mental stresses that might have been left over from the preceding days. If you happen to have the pleasure of making love somewhere in between waking up and getting up, the morning wake up is complete.

Being by myself, I climb back into bed and am left with my own thoughts. I try to get right back into the same spot that I had just vacated. Too late - the spot had already cooled and I could feel the heat from my body being drained into the bed's mattress. Knowing that it was too late, I got up and peeked into the next room to see if there was any action going on.

There was no one in the living area of the suite so I walked over to the second bedroom and cracked open the room door ever so slightly. No one there either. Scanning the room, the bed was made and everything in place as if no one had been there at all that night. There was a slight, but distinct, distasteful odor in the room that smelled of sweat and sex. I know the odor and what it comes from. I am about to close the door of the room when I notice a Trojan lubricated sensitive condom package right beside the room's trashcan. A smile crosses my face. Someone was a bad shot and missed the can. Daryl got lucky and was safe.

Closing the door back, I gathered myself and walked over to the balcony door, opened it and stepped outside. It was warmer outside than in the room but it was not the stifling heat that had greeted us when we had gotten off the plane - it felt good. The heat was a stark contrast to the cool bed that had been draining my body heat just minutes before. The warmth revived my body. I eased my stiff body down into the lounge chair that was on the balcony. The sun was just beginning to come up.

Looking up into the early morning sky, right before my eyes, I was treated to an array of color that often goes unnoticed by most. The sky was filled with clouds that reflected vivid shades of bronze, sand, and rust. It was picture perfect. It's funny, the sunrise was there all the time. I had never appreciated it before. Out on Lake Michigan in Chicago, courting a honey, after having done God knows what during the night, as a young man, it was not uncommon to go to the boat to cap off the night.

Most people look at having a boat as being outside of their reach. It's as easy as one, two, and three. That is three friends who understand that being common just won't get it if you're going to be a mover and shaker in the windy City. Thirty or forty feet will do fine.

No experience is necessary considering that the boat, most likely, will not leave its dock more than once or twice in a season. During those times you can hire someone who really knows how to handle the boat. Just think, you have a million dollar client out on the boat trying to close a real estate deal. If you can't handle the boat masterfully, does the client start to question what else you don't know how to handle? Remember, stay within your element and shine with the things that you do well. The things that you don't do well, pay someone to do them. Most times you can still take the credit or most of it anyway.

Rent the boat for the season. It is not that expensive when the cost is split between three people. Right away the buzz on the street will be Dee's boat have you seen it; been on it; how big is it; how many does it sleep. I can't tell you how to run your life but the less that you tell people the more that they will use their imagination. How you got the boat, how much it costs, etc. is you and your partner's business alone.

One of the best places to dock the boat is at River City. River City is an apartment complex that also has a marina, store, doorman, security, and a friendly marina manager who understands thirty people on your boat at three in the morning. The great thing about it is that your boat is parked dockside and not hooked up to a buoy in the middle of nowhere requiring a small row boat to get to it.

Imagine after three or four drinks trying to convince someone to get in a wobbly row boat to get out to your 'boat - ain't happening. River City's marina provides you with the ability to walk right up to your boat and get right in. The boat has three cabins, thus timing with the other renters is not an issue. Strawberries and a bottle of Crystal and it's on.

Viewing the sunrise through your date's eyes is the kind of nightcap that sets you apart from the rank and file. During the day, the boat is an excellent diversion -just right to invite selected friends, family, and clients. The summer days for the boat are split between the renters. With good friends it works fine. A firm understanding must be had between the renters not to let others have the boat, not your mother, under any circumstances.

Having seen many sunrises in the past, the uncertainty of the future made this one touch me in a way that one has never affected me before. Just then an Elton John song came to mind and I started humming.

"Someone save my life tonight... I'm sleeping with myself tonight - thank God I'm still alive. "

* * *

Daryl put his key card in the door and tried to push it open quietly. Clothes disheveled and a guilty look on his face, he was happy to see the room was empty. Flopping his three hundred plus pounds onto the couch, Daryl could not believe that the two girls were game for everything. Was it wrong to give them a little something so that they could get back to Los Angeles? We had left the party and came back to the suite.

They tried to make me choose between the two of them. When I couldn't decide, they offered to let me try them both. They were like night and day; Heather had to be at least six feet tall, black as a moonless night, shapely legs that never ended. I guess you can't be born with everything; what looked like her natural hair was a weave that almost came off in my hand.

Beth, clearly of mixed descent, was the color of a brown paper bag. Her hair was cut short in a Nia Long style that foretold of her sassy attitude. About five foot even, with a small butt, a small waist, short legs, with a perfect - not surgically altered - chest. They must be lovers themselves because they worked perfectly together.

Beth had a briefcase, that we stopped at her car to get out of her trunk, that was filled with jells and toys. When we got back to the room someone had set things up since all of our suitcases were gone, the lights turned down low, and music playing on the box. I glanced over at the room safe - it was closed and locked. With that, I knew that my boys took care of things and I relaxed a bit.

Heather made herself comfortable at the mini bar while Beth started searching around her briefcase. The first thing that she pulled out of her case was a natural sponge. During the continuing dialog of small talk, she went over to the wet bar and drew some temperate warm water into a small plastic bowl. She added a bit of cherry scented oil to the bowl that foamed when the sponge was dipped and wrung in it.

As Beth was getting her water ready, Heather tore herself from the mini-bar to, as she put it, "get me ready." In a voice that sounded like she swallowed an old man, she started calling me "Big Daddy."

Normally, I think that this would have turned me off but the sound of it easing off of her tongue, through the small gap between her two front teeth, and past her juicy, deep purple colored, action packed lips sounded of pure sex. Off went my shirt to a soft moan of "Big Daddy" which made the unbuckling of my belt and removal of my pants take place without my notice.

It's never a good underwear day when you need it to be - the elastic in my faded XXXL blue Calvin Cline boxers was all but non-existent and the taking off of my pants caused my drawers to be at my ankles. I would like to think that it was my stiff erection that made the next "Big Daddy" rumble out of Heather's lips and not my slightly oversized stomach.

Beth, armed with her sponge proceeded to begin a sponge bath of me. She had removed her clothes down to her bra and panties. Small and compact, not cut up or anything, just everything in the right place. Her matching bra and panties perfectly contrasted her skin tone. She opened her legs wide and while standing up straddled me and started to drip sudsy water slowly onto my chest.

Looking up, I could see that her panties were little strings of fabric - what a view. While looking, I heard the hum of an electric appliance in the background. I glanced over and saw Heather using a ladies cordless razor on her shapely leg. Beth kneeled down on her knees at the head of the bed and put her warm sex on the top of my bald head. I felt her heat, softness, and wetness on top of me. Not letting a second of time or one sensation end before the next one began, she took her sponge and started in on one of my nipples - "Oh, my God."

While I was trying to recover from the sensations that are making me wish that today would never end, Heather started to groom my pubic hair. This virgin growth had never seen a razor before which intensified my reaction that included "what the..." My reaction caused Beth to smile and console me with a reminder that Heather was still just trying to get me ready.

The razor's blade didn't hurt - it was just cold. She started at the right knee and proceeded up to my waist. Up from the left knee to up around my dick. I was becoming hairless in all the right places and I didn't want it to stop.

After being shaved in the front, I was sponged off by Beth. I noticed that she paid special attention to my penis. I suspect that she was looking for imperfections that any type of venereal disease would leave. No lesions, no warts, or excretions being present, I must have passed the inspection since the bath continued. Soon thereafter, I was turned over onto my stomach.

I was shaved from the back of the knee on up to my waist. Oh yes - my ass was shaved. When one of my cheeks was lifted and the razor got close to my hole, I decided that enough was enough and I hoped that down there did not stink. Calming any fear that I might have, I was sponged off there too.

Safe sex was my motto for the evening. Five condoms later, I was being fondled by Beth and had to say "No more." I'm just one man. Having spent a lot of energy, my mind turned to steak and eggs. Food being a strong weakness that I have, I asked the girls how did a little breakfast sound?

At breakfast, I learned that the girls were stranded here and trying to get back to Los Angeles and I offered to help. Of course, breakfast was on me and through the cash station machine I found one hundred dollars to give to them to make sure they got home.

* * *

I came off of the balcony into the suite to find Daryl lounging on the couch with a shit-eating smile on his face. I woke him out of his fantasy by asking him what was going on with Al and Len. His response of, "I don't know, I haven't seen them," did not surprise me.

AI, I knew would not lose a lot of money because he is a miser. However, Len is a different subject altogether. I was not too worried - Vegas has this effect on people. The first night you spend partying and gaming. The casino does everything to keep you there all night. Good free drinks, friendly dealers, good piped-in music, a good looking girl bringing you cigars and cigarettes for free if you like, a little extra oxygen pumped in to keep you wide awake, followed by good coffee, before you know it the sun is coming up.

"Yo, Daryl, what's up boy? How did it go with the two hotties?"

"Dee, it was a good time but nothing really happened. You know how it is when you just meet someone a lot of talking and what have you."

"Come on man - do I look like I just fell off of a beet truck or something? I know something happened."

"Nothing serious, they both came back to the room, a few drinks and a lot of talking that's all."

"So you didn't have to use any of the twenty pack of condoms that I know you brought with you?"

"It was fun Dee, but you know how it is."

Some brothers are like that. They are so insecure that you are going to find fault in what they are doing that they will do anything to hide the truth. I thought Daryl and I were past this point of judging one another. I was ready to ask the question that inquiring minds wanted to know. After our setup did he find out that they were professionals. "Do you think that they were prostitutes?"

"Naw man - why would you say that. Oh, just because I pulled them they had to be prostitutes. See Dee, it's not like that..."

He was still talking as he left the room; I think mainly to convince himself. The door was closed - slammed hard - and I could still hear him talking. His demeanor told on him. He was all up in one of them if not both of them. The thought of them being prostitutes is hitting him hard right now.

Maybe we should not have set him up like that. Some guys just are not ready for reality. The bad part is that he's lying to me and lying to himself-anyone could see that those girls were in it for the money. Good thing for the room safe or we all could have lost last night.

* * *

That Dee is an asshole. If it's not about him, he has to find fault in it. Dammit - I thought I had cleaned in here good. What the hell is this condom wrapper doing still here, he thought to himself as he picked it up and shoved it into his front pocket. I have never paid for sex in my life and I didn't start last night. Well, I guess when you really look at it nothing is ever free. When you send the flowers, pay for the candy, dinners, and gifts, I guess you always pay something. No way were those girls prostitutes - no way.

Chapter 11
Dee's Past Haunts Him

My plan for the day was to get a little R & R. I wasn't hungry but the medicine I had to take each morning could not be taken on an empty stomach or I would get sick. Many times, I cheat and drink a glass of milk with the pills and that does the trick. I don't want anything to go wrong on Friday and Saturday so I think I will go down and get something to eat. The rest of the morning I'm going to spend out at the pool.

Just then, Daryl came out of the room. He had calmed down and was starting some small talk and asking what my plans were for the day. I told him about the pool and he said that was a great idea, he didn't get a lot of rest last night and laying around the pool was about all that he could handle. Then out of the blue, for some reason he asked me if I thought I would ever get married again.

"Married? You were there the last time I had a wedding, right? Trust me, you will be there if and when I have another one."

Daryl bringing up his wedding sent Dee to thinking about his try at getting married. As a very young man, of course I fell in love. Her name was Phelma – everybody called her Dude. Dude was a name that stuck with her since grade school because back then she was such a tomboy. Moreover, as she began to get older she did not have an affinity for her first name. She hated the name Phelma.

I met Dude as a second semester freshman at Northern. She was great. She came from a good home, had the softest way about herself, and she loved me to death. After a few trying times and the fraternity pulling at me, our relationship solidified. Over the next four years she stood by and let me do my thing as long as I didn't disrespect her.

After graduating, the next logical step in a young man's life is to get married. Whether or not our dreams and wants were headed in the same direction, if we wanted children, how many, when, strength of credit, and other things were never talked about. We were on our way down the aisle on the strength of love.

With no notice to Dude, I went to Jeweler's Row on Wabash Street in the heart of the Loop in downtown Chicago. Jeweler's Row is a section of downtown Chicago that has jewelers lined up and down the street- it caters mostly to the Chicago area jewelry novices. There are many good shops and just as many that the buyer has to beware of. I went in one shop and came out with an SI quality two-carat, marquee cut, princess setting diamond engagement ring. It was gorgeous. With ignorance being bliss, it didn't matter to me that I probably paid twice as much as I should have for the ring. I was happy and ready to ask the question.

I picked up Dude at about eight o'clock p.m. from the Beverly area on Chicago's southwest side. We headed east on 99th street onto the Dan Ryan expressway to the Congress Drive exit. A few stoplights later I made a left onto Columbus and found a parking space. We got out of the car and started walking.

It was a fall evening and the temperature by Lake Michigan had started to fall and it was getting cool. I put my arm around her to keep her warm and we walked like two lovers for the three blocks that it took to get to Buckingham Fountain. We got there at about 8:45. I had told Dude that I was supposed to meet a friend down there and we were going for a late dinner.

Dude was absolutely beautiful. She was blessed with golden skin that captured light and reflected it back to you. As tall as me in her heels her reddish-brown hair had natural highlights that caught my eye. She had deep brown eyes that were full of life and rimmed by the longest eye1ashes that I had ever seen. A thin, lean body that most black men would say was lacking, but one that time would fill out and be perfect; especially after a few children.

She was the type of woman whose presence and class were obvious. Not one person ever asked why I was getting married; one look at her and it was clear.

At nine o'clock sharp the fountain exploded with an array of color intermixed with different heights of water. The water and colors were in a constant state of flux that at once entranced the eye.

With a backdrop of color, in front of the crowd that gathers daily for the light and water show, I got down on both knees and started serenading my love with a song from my high school days by Michael Henderson. The song just came to mind.

"All was not lost today - your brown eyes converted me, and let me know that you're the right girl for me. You don't need two, it's the same love I offer you. It would be a shame if you let someone else take my place. You've got me dreaming - I can't turn without you being there. So stop this mistreating of me I want to stay; I want to lay and just be your man. Oh, please be my girl... "

The crowd was paying more and more attention to my antics and Dude was getting embarrassed. With that, I got the ring out of my pocket and took her left hand and tried to slip the ring onto her ring finger. Her reaction was to pull back slightly. Holding my ground, I didn't let go of her hand and the ring was on. I looked into her eyes and without my saying a word she said yes. The crowd went wild with applause.

Dinner that night was off because all she wanted to do was go home and show and tell to her family. It was a good day and I was truly happy and she was too. That happy feeling was one to hold onto because after that things started moving fast. She wanted a big wedding. She wanted this; she wanted that. I really didn't want any of it, so my attitude was indifferent and that she hated.

Days turned into a month and months into a year and before I knew it the wedding was a month away. With that, I had to change my ways and tell the two other women that thought I was theirs; I was getting married.

Sandra was first, it was my twenty-fourth birthday - July 3 - less then a month before the wedding date of August 2. Sandra wanted to come by the apartment to bring me a gift. I knew what the gift was. I had dropped a few hints about my lay-a-way at Marshall Field's. She came by my apartment that was on the third floor of a three flat brownstone on the city's southeast side.

This girl was in no way pretty but she was hot as hell. She had straw-like sandy brown hair. She was a decent looking light-skinned woman but her teeth had shifted when she was pregnant with her daughter and her mouth was jacked.

For me our relationship was about sex. She flat out turned me on. There was never a time when we made love only once in a night. It was always at least three - if not more. She always came and most times together with me. It was a physical and mental high to be with her.

Just like I thought, she had the suit. Trying to do the right thing, I had to tell her to take the suit back to the store. I told her that we had to end things and she started crying. I really liked her and hated hurting her. There was nothing that I could do - I had to tell her. Trying to console her, I found myself hugging her. Hugging her led to me rubbing her back. Rubbing her back led to... Before I knew it, we were in the bed and I was so hard that the first time I came I just kept going.

Four hours later, we finished our conversation and it was over. As she was leaving I reminded her to take the suit. I walked her down to her car; her tears were unbearable. I felt like a jackass and I was one. I wanted to reach out to her and explain my actions. There was no explanation that was good enough to explain an insensitive ass's actions; I tried to hand her the suit. She turned away from me and said, "Keep it."

Beverly, whom I had been going out with as long as I had Dude, was different. Like Sandra, she was sexy but she was also fine as fine can be. My boys and I nicknamed her Picasso because her body was like a work of art. Oh, my god, she was all that and a bag of chips. Thinking back, the only reason that I chose Dude over her was that her family background was better.

Beverly was one hundred eighty degrees apart from Sandra. With her it was all about the sex. She was working me every time that she could because the sex was good. She was using me and being a naive little boy I could not see it. When I told her she grabbed her Gucci bag and was out without a word. It was over.

My boys had a slamming bachelor party for me - three women doing some of the unthinkable. For some reason, I just didn't want to be there. It's the day before the wedding and I knew that I was making a mistake. Up to now, I wasn't man enough to stop it. I stayed up all night and tried to explain things to Len.

We ate breakfast at about 4:00 a.m. at the House of Pancakes on Western Avenue. When it was over, I told him that I needed to be alone. I walked the streets trying to get my head together. At 8:00 a.m. I was at Ed's Style World to get my hair cut. Ed wasn't open, but he let me in anyway. I have been getting my hair cut at Ed's Style World by Ed himself, since I was ten years old. Over the years he had seen me grow from a child to a young man. While he was cutting my hair, I confided in him.

"Ed, I'm supposed to get married today."

"Ah, that's good young blood, the hair cut is on the house today."

"I'm not sure if I should get married. I thought that I would be happy but I'm not and now I'm locked in."

"Young Blood, nobody can tell you what to do but your heart. If it doesn't feel right, don't do it - bottom line."

"I just don't know, Ed."

Ed was the only one who said not to do it. The only one to see through all of the muck and give me an answer with some substance.

Everyone else who had a view came up with answers that were clouded, including mine, based upon how things would look to the outside world.

I finished up with Ed and caught a cab back downtown to Dude's and my new apartment. At the apartment, I went through the situation over and over again in my head. It was clear that my womanizing had not prepared me to be ready to get married. The only question was if I could straighten myself out and go through with the wedding.

Three hours before the wedding, I was still alone at my apartment and, in spite of all of the advice that I had gotten, still uncertain about what I should do. I decided that a brisk run might clear my mind. I went for a three mile run though the neighborhood. Why would I listen to my barber?

I ran east on Polk to State. Over to Congress and made a beeline to Lake Shore Drive. The lake was just the setting for some real soul searching thoughts. By the time I got to Lake Shore Drive and Monroe, I knew what I was going to do. I retraced my run and arrived back at the apartment about an hour and forty-five minutes before the event was to kick off.

I did the three S's in record time. I got dressed, hopped into my Mazda RX7, and was on my way to Holy Faith Baptist Church. A man on a mission, I broke every rule of the road in record speed getting to the church.

Daryl was the first one to meet me at the door of the church. "Dee, where in the hell have you been? Do you know that everybody was scared wondering where you were? I knew when you had that trifling Len as your best man that something like this would happen."

"Look Daryl, I need to talk to Dude. You need to find her and if she doesn't want to see me before the wedding, at least get her to a phone where I can talk to her - it's urgent Daryl."

"What's going on Dee? You're not going to do what I think you are - are you? No, no, no you're not."

"Daryl, this is not about you. It's not about anyone except Dude and me. Its not about who's going to think what or say what. I'm past caring about them. This is my future - can you do what I asked you to do or do I have to do it myself?" Damn, that boy is so in everybody's business. Why can't people give you opinions when you ask for them and keep them when you don't?

I waited for Dude in a back room off of the church's kitchen. The invites to the wedding were starting to arrive. It was only twenty minutes before the wedding was to start when Dude came storming into the room dressed in a pair of jeans and a red tee shirt.

"What the hell is going on Dee? Daryl is back there talking like the wedding is off or something." Standing there, Dude looked like everything that any man could ever ask for in a bride.

Great, Daryl being the busy body that he is has removed any doubt of what I was going to do with his big mouth. “Baby, I do love you so much but I'm just not sure. Not sure that I'm half the man that my grandfather was. Not sure that I can be what a husband should be. I have not been the type of boyfriend, fiancé, or friend that one could be proud of, so I don't have a base to ensure that I can be a good husband.”

The air was filled with a still like I never felt before. Needing the air to stir I continued, “I'm not sure and I question if I should take the next step. I want to be a good man and do the right thing. There is so much that I want for us, but I also don't want to make you unhappy.”

“Just say it Dee. If you want to call things off, embarrass the hell out of me in front of all of these people, then just say it. I can't believe this is happening to me.”

“Dude this is the hardest thing that I've ever had to do in my life. All I have to base my decision on is that I believe that men make decisions and the only bad decision is not making one at all. If you find that you have made a bad decision as a man, you have to change your direction. Dude, as a man I just can't get married on this day.”

“Well Dee, if not today then never - you hear me never!”- As she spoke to me, she was walking towards me with what I believed was a fair amount of hate in her eyes. I looked down to the floor to avoid her eyes just before the stars took over my head. She had knocked fire from me with a slap to the face that originated on the East Coast.

From that day forward, I never needed more than one woman at a time. If I started dating you can bet that I have mentally left all past loves behind. Dude's and my parting was so bitter that I never was able to tell her or her family how much they meant to me. They were my Chicago family. They were all I had and when I tore myself from my marriage to Dude, I lost all of them and I was truly lost.

For the first time in my adult life, there was not a love interest in my life. I hated the feeling and I vowed never to make a mistake with love again. It was about me. Dude never let me close enough to her to share her pain. For the longest time I waddled in mine. Not having access to her or her family any longer and feeling like the world was going to end, I wrote a letter to Dude.

July 31

Dear Dude,

By the time you get this letter I can only hope that you have been able to reconcile my betrayal of your faith, your heart, your trust. The one thing that I want you to be sure of is that it was not about you. Any man would be blessed to have you as his wife. I just wasn't worth the time and effort that you put into me. I didn't truly know within myself that I was not right until I tried to be right. I do love you...

The letter went on for four pages and for the first time it was not enough to calm the emotions within.

Chapter 12
Dee Gets a Little Rest and Relaxation

Armed with a pair of black Speedo swim/run trunks, not the kind of trunks that reveal everything that you have, but the kind that are meant for running and swimming in. They leave just enough to the imagination that a woman wants to see a bit more - a red tank top that is not so tight that it makes one look like he is showing off, but if someone wants to see how hard you have worked out in the past they can - and a pair of black flip-flops - I head down to the hotel pool. I take with me enough money and enough suntan lotion to last for an entire day of fun and frolic in the sun.

As I was leaving the room, Len and Al were just making it in from the night before. They were trying to outdo each other in volume as they were bragging about the women that were coming on to them and how much money they had won. Between the two of them, they had won just a little more than one hundred fifty dollars. A sum that to me was not worth the thirty plus hours that the two of them had been up since waking to fly into town the day before.

Knowing how it feels to have someone rain on your parade, I caught their excitement even though I did not feel it. It's like a line in the poem, *Test of a Man.* “It takes a man to stand and cheer as the other fellow stars.” I was truly happy for my friends but it just was “been there, done that” for me.

Before I continued down the hall to the elevator, I told Len and Al that I was on my way down to the pool and that they should come down after they got some rest. They said that they would, but I knew that as tired as they had to be, it would be hours before they would be fit enough to enjoy the sun, sights, and relaxation that the pool atmosphere offered.

Down the elevator I went. Before going out to the pool area, I stopped and bought a turkey sandwich on a croissant from the casino's deli. The sandwich was tasteless to me but I wolfed it down anyway. After I ate the sandwich, I took the three pills that I needed to take with a cup of ginger ale.

I was all good and ready to walk out to the pool. As I exited the hotel, on my way to the pool, I was met by the hotel's wildlife. No, really. The hotel has a flock of flamingos and African Penguins that are entertaining the people on their way to the pool. To everyone's delight, the African Penguins look just like the cold weather penguins that you are used to seeing. The only difference is that these can withstand the heat of the desert.

The wildlife roaming adds a good touch to the well-manicured hotel grounds and enhances the feeling that you are indeed on vacation - mostly because you are seeing something that you don't see everyday. The tourists are taking picture after picture to memorialize the moment. The hotel's return visitors are in that "been there, done that" mode and move swiftly to the pool that is about one hundred yards away from the wildlife. I pause to see if there is anything worth seeing over there before I continue to the pool. Hey, old habits die hard.

The pool is very large with about three sections. It seems that the people in the pool have sectioned off areas to meet their needs. One section is for family type fun. It has pool slides and lots of activity taking place. There's another section that seems to be filled with men and women who are on the prowl. People in this area are there to have as much interaction with the other sex as possible in the shortest amount of time. Tall, short, lean, fat, tattooed, augmented, etc., you name it, it's there. The other section seemed just to be a calm crowd that wanted sun. I just wanted a place to hang out and I found it. The section that I was in had a waterfall that if you swim out to and stand under it, you get the best back relaxation that you can imagine. About forty-five seconds under there and you are relaxed enough to just layout. It's a genuinely great feeling. The pool has a pool bar that encompasses everything that one needs to relax if you are apprehensive of the water, for whatever reason, and don't want to get in the water.

The pool bar is already filled with people and it is only 10:30 a.m. The people were not drunk or anything -just having fun with music, conversation, and light drinking. For the price of ten dollars, you can order a half yard glass of a mostly ice and juice novelty drink. After two of them, the sheer size of them will take you at least an hour to drink, you are still as sober as you were when you first started drinking. Between the sun, the pool, the half naked girls, and the drinks, it's a great way to spend the afternoon.

Today, I'm not here for the girls, only the R&R. I flash my room key at the cabana boy and secure two beach towels to lay on the pool chair. I have my drink already so I proceed to find a pool chair that offers sun and sights. I prefer to be right next to the pool where I can jump in the water when I feel the need. Suntan lotion, a *Men's Health* Magazine, a *Gentlemen's Quarterly* Magazine, my cell phone, and I am ready for my day.

* * *

Needing what I needed, I fell asleep by the pool. The sound of my cell phone chiming woke me. I have a Nokia Personal Communicator that allows me to stay connected no matter where I am. The phone has call waiting, caller ID, voice mail, Internet capacity, voice and numeric paging, e-mail, and even an alarm clock. What did I ever do before I got it? It was Lisa on the phone.

"Hello" I always answer the phone like I am surprised at who is on the other end. I don't want everyone to know that I have caller ID on my cell phone. When people know that you have it, it starts them to wondering, when you don't answer your phone, if you are screening your calls and avoiding them.

"Yes, baby, I'm fine. How are you? ... Yeah, I know that you're worried about me. You know that I'm taking care of myself - that's what this trip is all about - taking care of things once and for all ... Me too. Are you ready for Friday? ... You know those morning flights always leave on time so that they can make their connections with other flights and so the plane can be where it needs to be later in the day ... I'm sorry. I'm not trying to tell you how to fly, but remember you are flying with your friend that thinks the entire world revolves around her. She is liable to be an hour late and then ask the gate attendant why they didn't hold the plane for her ... I know that you will be on top of her ... What? ... That's great Lisa; what does that make? Ninety-two pounds so far, right? Who would have thought? I am so proud of you girl; you know that don't you? So you have reached your goal and it's just maintenance now ... I took them and all I am doing now is relaxing out by the pool. I might have overdid it a bit with the sun, though. I'm going to turn over and try and even out ... Okay, I will call you tonight. Lov ya. Bye."

Chapter 13
Dee Meets Lisa

I've known Lisa for about five years. I met her mother in a Black Studies seminar where I was asked to speak. We began an intellectual dialog concerning current events that continued for about two years. About a year after we started corresponding, she began trying to set up a blind date with Lisa and me for about six weeks. I told her that I did not like blind dates and she always said that she understood. The next time I saw her she was back at it again. "Don't worry, it is not a date - just a dinner party with my husband, some friends, and I think my daughter will be there. You know you guys would make a cute couple."

Mrs. Lewis had a way of twisting your arm without it hurting by using her accent and the inflection of her voice. So I said "yes" to her dinner party but made it clear that dinner was all I was saying yes to. I should have known that it was a setup all along.

I rang the Lewis doorbell on the night of the party dressed to the nines. I had a bottle of Rosemont Estates Shiraz wine to present to the hosts of the party. When the door opened, I must have looked just like a blind date. Surely, with the way that Mrs. Lewis duped me, I was blind. Lisa informed me that her parents were still up at their cabin in Wisconsin and could not make it back for dinner. She smiled and told me that she hoped that her cooking would be okay.

My God – if I could only have back the last five minutes. I could get out of here. I wanted to be invisible. Lisa was, oh, about five foot in height, oh, about five feet wide, and oh, about five feet thick. Her hair, pulled back in a frizz ball of a ponytail, was down to the middle of her back. If that was not bad enough, I've seen clowns with better makeup. I silently wished to be invisible again. No luck.

I found the only common ground that I wanted to find that day. Lisa and her family had an over four hundred volume compact disk collection. The CDs were sorted by artist and a quick perusal revealed that the family had a love for jazz. I picked out a dated Michael Franks "Skin Dive" CD and put it in. I proceeded to pick out ten other CDs, mostly smooth jazz that I wanted to listen to.

When Lisa came into the room we started talking music. This girl knows her music history. We ate, talked, drank wine, and listened to music for half the night. It was good.

We were bonding and becoming close as friends.

* * *

I like this guy. He even likes music - how lucky can a girl get? Mama was right, he is to die for, were Lisa's thoughts. Unlike many women, Lisa was not spoiled by the plethora of attention that is routinely given to a good looking woman. The overabundance of attention in many cases changes the attitudes of many women to one that feels that men owe them something on the basis of their looks.

While many young women were being courted, Lisa had her face buried in a book solidifying her future. Being an honor roll student each of her four years at Whitney Young High School was followed up by a full ride scholarship to the University of Illinois at Champagne/Urbana. Four years on the Dean's list and graduating with the highest honors did not change the fact that success comes with a price.

The price for Lisa was the fact that there were no boys lined up to meet the girl that thought that it was more important to study than to fix her hair, do her nails, wear the latest styles, learn the latest dances, or be seen with the right people in the right places. Lisa spent her time working on her base, a base that would mean success in her future.

Unlike Lisa's, for many backs tomorrow's success is questionable. Not having a foundation for success, trying to make up for years of missed education is all but impossible except for the extremely gifted student. Lisa endured the price one pays for years of neglecting social norms - not the norms you learn from a book, but what you learn from the everyday interaction with people your own age. Doing what young people do is hard to make up. Her lifestyle of not caring about those norms had transformed a fairly attractive woman into a two hundred nine pound woman who could do nothing with her hair or her lack of style.

Lisa was born to a white mother Mary Beth from England who fell for a black air force captain John E. Lewis while he was on a tour there. The captain at twenty-five years of age was experiencing his first exposure to white people who were not prejudged against him before they knew him, because of his skin color. It's not that these types of people don't exist in the United States; it's just that being from a small southern town, Thula, Mississippi, did not lend itself to one experiencing progressive thinking from his white neighbors from across town.

In the five years that he attended Fisk University, a predominately black college, there was little or no exposure to the expectations of white society. From Fisk, John went right into the military. It's clear how the norm could seem out of the norm and how a college educated man could go through twenty-five years of life and not be exposed to the common ground that exists between people of every nationality and race. The acceptance that John received in

England engulfed him mind, body, soul, and spirit. Race was not an issue.

Mary Beth, being from a small village in England, was never taught to hate people that were different from her. When she met John at the Officer's Club, she embraced what they had in common and the differences did not matter. Liking the same music was the first common theme. Mary's strong desire to visit the United States let her feed on John's stories on life in the States. In her mind anything that was said on the negative side about the States was twisted into something idyllic and acceptable.

John's overseas tour was coming to an end when he found out that Mary was pregnant. As expected by the military, if you got a woman in a family way, John married Mary Beth.

For the next five years they enjoyed the relative safety that is afforded on a military base. Staying on coastal bases that had an element of readiness associated with them, it was easy to find men and women who understood that no matter the color, I am my brother's keeper. War and stress have a way of breaking down all of the misconceptions that people have with race. When there is a chance that the guy next to you will have to save your life one day, race goes out of the window and good people prevail.

When John's military career came to an end, going back to Thula was out of the question. Since he had left, race relations in Thula had not progressed to a point that a black man with a white wife and a mixed child could feel safe there. Additionally, Mary still had not grown accustomed to the divisions that lay between the races in the United States. She would routinely get into heated idealist conversations with others about how things should be.

Even with John, after being exposed to life outside of Mississippi, it was questionable if he would be mentally able to conform to the unwritten laws of the state that kept blacks in their place. Clearly, settling back in Thula was not an option.

The threesome settled in nicely in a western suburb of Chicago called Oak Park. Oak Park is a race makeup controlled suburb that ensured that white flight did not occur by limiting the number of black families that could move into the area. While other nearby suburbs experienced an exorcist of the neighborhood, Oak Park stood tall as a model of racial harmony. It was also a safe haven for mixed couples in a metropolitan area that was largely segregated. Mary loved the area and the area embraced her and her unique way of speaking.

Mary loved the states but never fully understood the divisions that exist between the different cultures in the states. Not wanting her daughter to become another minority that never met her potential, she made sure that Lisa understood the importance of her education. With an education, the opportunities were beyond belief and beyond anything that she could have expected in her small village back home in Europe.

She imparted into her daughter Lisa, to take advantage of all the opportunities that are available to her. Mary was a stay-at-home mom. She took time to educate herself on the struggle of black people in America. From the books, movies, and people that she spoke with it became apparent to her that her husband an educated well spoken black business man was an anomaly and not the norm.

She wanted the world for her daughter and her research made it clear to her that Lisa's hair and skin tone may be a barrier to her. It seemed that the only thing that she could do was to make sure that her daughter took her education seriously. From the time that Lisa started talking, she was drilled with education. Educational programs, educational toys, after school programs, etc. Failure was not an option.

There was no time for the fun things in life and Lisa did not miss what she never had. There was none of the balance that social interaction brings or the fitness that simple childhood play brings. Without these things, Lisa became an introverted two hundred nine pound woman who was ready for the finer things in life but had no idea how to get them.

* * *

"Oh it's getting late, I'd better be going. Lisa I had a great time. Maybe we can do something like this again?"

"Let me get your coat." *What should I do? I can't just let him slip out of here.* "So Dee, when are we going to do something like this again?"

"I don't know, but let me give you my number and we can go from there. How does that sound?"

“Okay, that will have to do.”

During the year, the two of them became close friends. It never went any further because Dee would not let it. Since it was only a friendship, weight was never an issue with Dee. Since it was only a friendship, Lisa's affair with food and music continued; weight was not an issue.

Chapter 14
Lisa and Dee Become Friends

During hard times you look for the familiar. Things that have provided comfort in the past that you know are safe. It was during one of these times that I became closer to Lisa. We were buddies. The type of friends that could see a movie together and get something to eat and have no strings attached, just good clean fun. Hour upon hour was spent explaining small cultural nuances to her that she came across during her day. She was really a sheltered person.

I had just received some life altering news and was contemplating not meeting Lisa to go to the movies as we had planned. Trying to face things head on, I met her anyway. For some reason, I opened up to her and she said that she would be there for me. I knew that she would.

Over the next few days we spent time together. I took a leave from work to concentrate on my issues so I had all kinds of time to just hang out. Lisa was remodeling her basement apartment in her parent's Oak Park home. Always good with my hands, I offered to put down a ceramic floor in her kitchen. Since I didn't do this kind of work everyday, it was a slow process.

Every night we would search for just the right things to put in the apartment; paint, tile, appliances, everything. It was fun. I got a chance to see Lisa as she really was; remodeling a living space, you really get to know a person. The thoughts that went with the decisions that she made were there for me to see.

We worked late into the night and I would stay the night on Lisa's couch. We would watch television together and comment on the programs. When all was said and done, I knew Lisa and Lisa knew me.

One Sunday we were out at the Sears Home Outlet store looking for a refrigerator. In the mall there was a T. J. Maxx Department Store that I wanted to stop in. I went into the store and Lisa hesitantly followed. I like to go into stores like T. J. Maxx to buy things like tee shirts and socks. There was a time that you could find some pretty good values at these kind of stores but nowadays the prices for shirts and other items are not that much of a bargain. For me T.J. Maxx is good for socks and underwear.

Going in to T. J. Maxx did something to Lisa. As she went down each aisle not finding anything that would fit her, she started to break down. I walked over to console her and it came to me that she was not as comfortable with her size as I thought she was. Over the years she had acted as if it was not an issue for her. We never talked about her weight and I had never considered how it must have affected her.

Her attire was generally a pair of sweats and gym shoes. Of course, her work attire included custom suits that fit her well and hid as much as possible. However, there is only so much you can do with fabric. For her, there were no in-between clothes; the type of clothes that you can put on and be stylish, comfortable, look sexy, and have fun in. No, for her it was just the sweats.

I could not get her to stop crying. I did my best to get her out of the store without causing too much of a scene. I got her into the car and back to her house. She had regained her composure and I was saying my goodbye, when Lisa
asked me to stay a little while longer and listen to a new Kenny Lattimore CD with her. After seeing her moments earlier broken down the way that she was, there is no way that I was going to say no to this simple request.

“Dee, I know that I am fat and out of shape but I just want someone to like and want me for me.”

“Hey, there's someone for everyone. You know that.”

“Dee, I've known you for over a year and a half and you have never once looked at me that way.”

"You're right; but it's not as if I don't like you. It's just that our friendship took a different direction. I stopped being the type of guy that ran a lot of women after I really let someone down and hurt them. I still can't believe that I was that person. It's not a good feeling at all. I don't want to start something that's not going to be right. I don't want to hurt anyone else. With my issues, what could I offer anyone?"

"Dee, I want you anyway that I can have you."

"What about as your friend?" I asked.. "Lisa you don't mean anyway that you can have me." I didn't wait for her response.

I didn't want a relationship with Lisa. However, I did care for her and her feelings. I went up to her and hugged her, a brotherly hug from my side. It was the first time that I had ever touched her. Through years of experience, a man learns a woman's reactions. Hers was tense and on the verge of another breakdown. Trying to comfort her, I let her stay in my arms and I let my mind drift. My mind drifted to Mary J. Blige's rendition of "Sweet Thing." I started singing softly to ease Lisa as well as myself.

"I'm a love you anyway you are. Even if you cannot stay, 1 think you are the one for me. Here is where you ought to be. I just want to satisfy you, though you're not mine, 1 can't deny you. Don't you hear me talking baby? Love me now or I'll go crazy. Sweet thang . . ."

She held onto me for dear life. I wasn't offering sex, just friendship, one friend comforting another. During the night I promised my friend and myself that I would help her. For the first time we had a conversation in earnest about her weight and looks.

I explained to Lisa, "Looks are something that most of us have to work on. Very few people have a look that can't be improved on.

Lisa had multiple issues, for one, her hair. She would wash it and pull it back into a long pony tail. By the time her hair dried there would be kinky strands of hair sticking out of her head. It must be that she doesn't know how to care for it. Her mother, being white, had no idea how to care for it. There were no relatives around to help Mary Beth out with her dilemmas on black hair. Lisa was the recipient of smooth facial skin that with a little attention was sure to shine.

After over a year of thinking that you know someone like the back of your hand, you find out that you really only know that part of them that they have allowed you to see. Over the years our interactions stayed in safe areas; areas that would otherwise rip us apart to the very core if they were ever treaded upon.

We had spent days talking about music, people, our jobs, sports - basketball being our favorite - and the like. Never did we reveal our souls. We did not place our flaws, insecurities, fears, and desires on the table for each other's private perusal. To do so might be to invite a critique from one who's off the cuff remark could break us unknowingly.

Tonight, the walls that kept us in those safe areas were falling, having been weakened over the past few weeks by all of the personal interaction between us. That night it was decided that the remodeling of her basement space would go in a different direction. The fifteen by twenty foot space that was going to be a music room, took a one hundred eighty degree turn. In the blink of an eye, my mind designed an exercise area to fit into the space. The space would be perfect to help my friend.

We kept the design of the room simple; a black padded floor, a mirrored wall, a universal machine, a heavy bag, dumb bells, an elliptical cycle, and a jump rope. Workouts were scheduled for six a.m. and six p.m. Monday through Friday - rain or shine.

At 5:45 the next morning the alarm on my phone woke me. I had spent the night again at Lisa's. I rolled off the couch and prayed that the clock was wrong. Lisa was already up and the smell of bacon was coming out of the kitchenette. I gained my bearings - I'm really not a morning person - and put on my black sweats.

The basement was cool and I needed the warmth that they would provide. Grandfather always said that the longest journey begins with the first decisive step. I was ready and now it's time to find out if Lisa was ready. Dressed and ready, I went into the kitchen and turned off the stove. I looked deep into Lisa's eyes and informed her that those days are over. Over her complaints, which included informing me that breakfast is the most important meal of the day, I dragged her into the exercise room. I had set up the room the night before. The boom-box was loaded with a tape I made of her favorite music. I turned on the box nice and low as not to alarm the rest of the house, and we were on.

* * *

Who in the shit does he think he is? Dammit, I'm picking up his habit of cursing. Up at six a.m. and can you believe it, he throws my food in the trash! I agreed to workout not diet. What was that anyway? He made me stand in the mirror and tell him what parts of my body I wanted to change. I felt like screaming, "Everything you moron! Everything!"

I have never been so embarrassed in my whole life - he inspected every part of my body. He measured everything - my neck, my shoulders, arms, chest, waist or should I say stomach, ass, thighs, and calves. You just can't imagine how it felt when he was writing it all down in a journal without saying a word. The nice guy that I trusted has turned into the biggest jerk that I've ever known - believe me at my size and weight I've know a few.

It took forty-five minutes to take my weight and measurements. Then he made me stand next to the mirror while he made an outline of my body with a thick black magic marker on the glass of the mirror - he outlined both front and side views of my body - like I don't know how I look. I can hear him now. "Walk in place" ... "Take your heart rate."... "Step up - step down." Over and over again. "Take your heart rate." Two hours - a total waste of my time. No breakfast and just enough time to shower and get to work.

Boy, I wish I could forget that shower. I was rushing and forgot to bring my baby powder into the bathroom with me. It's only two feet from the bathroom to the bedroom. I went for it. Yes, you guessed it he's standing right there looking at my naked body - eyes wide open - for what seemed like days. It was just a great way to start the morning.

* * *

That wasn't so bad. I found out where she is with her fitness. Not bad for someone her size. If looks could kill, I would have been dead three times over when I threw her bacon in the trash. It might not have been so bad if she didn't catch me sneaking a small piece of it into my mouth while I was throwing it away; her eyes went berserk. "Look I'm not the one in training" was all I could think to say. Why didn't I say something smart like sorry? She just stormed into her bedroom. On her way out of the door for work, I handed her a good sized Tupperware bowl of applesauce with some bran mixed in - a package of vitamins and a water bottle of grapefruit Juice.

The kicker was when I told her "nothing else before lunch. Okay?" Death was in her eyes so I quickly closed the door. Well tonight will be better. It had better be because from what I saw we have a long way to go. Three major rolls: the first one was where her chest was supposed to be, the second at her upper body, with a third one that hung low from her stomach down over her hip area. The Michelin tire man has nothing on her. We have a long way to go; I hope I can hold up. With her leaving for work, I got back on the couch - I wasn't feeling well.

Chapter 15
Dee Doing His Thing At the Pool

Just as I got turned over onto my stomach someone jumped into the pool and splashed water all over me. Damn, but it felt good so I just jumped in to cool off. It was about three o'clock and I thought another hour would do the trick. As I was getting out of the water, a twenty-something woman caught my eye as she was strolling my way. She had on a neon orange two piece suit by Body Glove. The front of her top was zippered and when you looked at it her full chest made you wish that she had it unzipped just a little more. Old habits die hard.

Noticing what I was doing, I resisted the temptation to check out her backside as she continued pass me. I wanted to look, but I also wanted to believe that I wasn't the dog that I used to be. I was saved by the emergence of Daryl and Al They were walking over to me and gawking at every girl at the pool over sixteen.

In front of me now, Daryl said, "What's up Dee?" They were standing right by my chair.

There were no empty chairs by where I was so after awhile they just kicked off their sandals and sat on the edge of the pool with their feet in the water.

"What have you guys been up to?" I inquired.

"Man, when I hit that bed I was O. U. T. out," Al replied. "Your boy here gangstered the second bedroom so I went into the room where you were last night."

"Yeah, but even with you in the room way across the suite, I could still hear you calling hogs. In fact, that's what woke me up. You know I need my beauty sleep," Daryl said patting his face as if he were a beauty queen or something.

"We're starving. You want to get something to eat?" Daryl inquired?

"Naw, I'll pass. Why don't you guys grab something and I'll meet you up in the room in a hour? I'll be finished down here by then. Where's Len?"

Al looked like the cat that ate the bird when he said, "I don't know." From his face I could tell that something was up. I didn't press it. I had the key to the room safe and most of his money and cards were in there, so how much trouble could he get into? As they were leaving to get something to eat, Ms. Neon Orange was back on the stroll headed my way.

Oh no eye contact. Instinctively I mouthed "hi" to her, acknowledging the fact that I knew that I was caught in her trap. She was Black and in her late twenties, probably in Vegas on vacation and wondering where the single brothers are that are promised in any vacation brochure.

Well, I hated to disappoint her but I was just not up for it.

"Hi, I'm Dee."

"I'm Kayla. Do you know that you're two toned?"

"Yeah, I kind of fell asleep on the front side so I need to work on the back. How's your tan coming?" She was dark enough that she could stay in the sun all day and get no darker.

"Very funny. As you can see I don't need a tan. Because of you, I might have one though," she playfully said while inspecting each of her arms. "What took you so long to say hi to me? I've been walking past you for at least an hour."

"Well alrighty then. I didn't notice until the last time you walked by. So what brings you to Vegas?" I calmly inquired.

"I just wanted to get away from the rat race of the work week. I decided to get away. My travel agent hooked me up with a flight here for a steal, so here I am. I've been here for two days and frankly, I'm a little disappointed. Where are all the brothers?! The only ones that I've seen so far are part of the help."

"Boy you really know how to deflate a brother's ego. So you just stopped by since you could not find any suitable brothers?"

"No, that's not it exactly. You are out here cooking yourself to look good are you not? If I didn't come over and tell you that you were doing a good job I wouldn't be doing my job would I?"

"I think I should say thank you, right? Anyway, what are you doing tonight? There are four of us here and I think hanging with us might be more fun than gambling the night away."

"Well, life is a gamble isn't it?"

With that we exchanged room numbers and set seven o'clock to touch base with each other. Len likes dark women. When he sees Kayla he's going to flip.

* * *

I was late getting up to the room. It was about five o'clock and the only one that was there was AI. He was knocked out on the couch with the television blasting. I turned off the television and went to the room and started setting out my gear for the evening. I chose a pair of black linen slacks and my black Kenneth Cole sandals. A silk blood red short sleeve Jhane Barnes shirt will be worn open and untucked over a black tee shirt. The warm weather mandates a soft clean scent. My current warm weather favorite is Issey Miyake. I'm ready. I feel a little dehydrated and I go to the room refrigerator and get a bottle of Dannon drinking water.

I sit back and reflect on how relaxed I am. If I had stayed in Chicago, I would have been a bundle of nerves right now. Breaking my routine has taken my mind off of the seriousness of the situation and provided much needed mental relaxation for me and the boys.

Lisa was the one who suggested that I get away. It was my idea to do it with the boys. I didn't want to hear any mouth about things so I just told them to come. They have no idea of the who, what, and why that surround us being here; they can just be natural with me instead of being all hyped up.

As I wait for the guys to make it in, I drink as much water as I can get down. It crosses my mind that I promised Lisa that I would call her before tonight. It's 3:36 here and that's 7:36 Chicago time. I think that I'll wait a little while before I call.

Chapter 16
Dee and Lisa Doing the Workout Thing

After a month of workouts, Lisa was starting to revolt. I took the scale out of the house and never gave her any indication of how she was doing. I just kept pressing her. I pressed especially hard in the area of her diet. Light morning meals that were always healthy. After her workout, I didn't want her to take in a lot of calories. Her body should supply the calories it needs after her workouts to maximize the effect of the workout. There is no eating after her 6:00 p.m. workout at all. Just as much water as possible.

The vitamins that she takes each morning are designed for someone who is working out and losing a lot of weight. They help her body use the food she eats in an efficient manner to the point that she needs less food. Her morning workout is basically a cardio workout with some floor work designed to work on her stomach areas.

Forty-five minutes on the elliptical cycle stepper. When we first started, she didn't have any resistance on the stepper and she could only do five minutes before her heart rate was too high for her to continue. After her second week, she was doing twenty minutes and sweating rivers.

We kept a water bottle of room temperature water right there so that she could keep herself hydrated. The water was room temperature to keep her from having the brain freeze that she often got when she drank cold water while working out. After just one month, she was up to forty-five minutes on the stepper, with a small amount of resistance, without any complaints.

After the elliptical cycle, we move to some floor work. So far the floor workout is limited to leg raises and crunches. Getting used to taking the time to work your abs is essential.

Bad workout habits are better off nipped in the bud since they have a tendency to fester. Most people have a habit of skipping their ab work. A great deal of your overall strength is derived from your mid-section. A strong mid-section promotes good posture and enhances your appearance. Attention to this detail, at an early age, continues to pay dividends throughout your entire life. It's easier to keep up than catch up. Right now the floor work is not paying off in the looks department, but in the future I'm sure it will.

We continue the workout session with about twenty minutes of jumping rope. The simplest exercises are sometimes the best. When we first started this exercise, Lisa was lucky to be able to skip over the rope twice. Now, about seven to ten times is the average length that she skips before she misses and has to start over again. Jumping rope is going to build her coordination and it is also one of the best aerobic exercises around. There are no excuses for not having a limited workout when you are on vacation. The rope fits into any carry-on bag and you don't need a special place to jump in.

The morning session ends with a short period of stretching. While stretching, Lisa has been in positions that she had never been in before. No jerking and trying to get her body to move in an unnatural way. Just a smooth pull to get the blood flowing to the tired muscles to promote flexibility and to keep from getting too sore from the workout. We have been getting it all done in about ninety minutes in the morning.

The evening workout is for strength and tone. Ten minutes on the stepper to get warmed up and then we attack a body part. We work arms, back, chest, shoulders, or butt and legs. Lisa had never worked out in her life.

During the first month we had to take it really easy. Her body is not used to the stresses that weight training placed on it. Sometimes the pain, when you are first starting this type of program, can be clear down to the bone. During the first month, one body part per day with a full seven day's rest in between. Until this week, I skipped working her legs altogether.

The pain that a good leg workout brings is almost debilitating the first time that you do it, or if you have laid off of it for a while. Thinking that it was more important to get her on a strong aerobic program, that included a lot of jumping and stepping, I put off working her legs for fear that the pain in her legs would stop her from doing her morning workout.

Near the end of the workout, twice a week, we hit the heavy bag. We take time to wrap her hands and put on bag gloves. I have taught her how to throw a punch and get the most out of the bag. Nothing intense just enough bag work to feel a whole upper body workout and have some fun taking out your built-up frustrations on something.

A few days ago was Lisa's first real leg workout. I warned her that there would be pain afterward and she said that she thought that she was up for it. We started out with some deep knee bends. They were done very low, controlled, and with no bouncing so that the strain to her knees would be minimized. A few lunges followed. Leg raises and toe raises were also included. Four sets of eight of each exercise with a little weight on the last two sets.

While she was doing the leg exercises, she was complaining that the exercises were too easy. I just said under my breath, "wait until tomorrow." Again the evening session ends with a short period of stretching, paying special attention to the areas that we just worked on.

A month into our exercise program, Lisa's untrained eye could not see the advances that she had made. Like many who start a program, when she didn't see her body turn into a Jada Pinkete like body in the month that she had been working out, caused her to lose faith and want to give up her fitness endeavors.

"Dee, there's nothing happening except my body feeling like a truck has run over it."

"I told you that your legs were going to hurt, didn't I? But you feel better than you did yesterday, right?"

"In certain places but my legs, my God, I can barely walk. I know that you told me that doing squats and lunges was going to hurt, but this is ridiculous. I can't even sit down and not feel the pain in my butt."

"I told you that once you get past this pain, it will never hurt like this again. Hey, no pain no gain. You know that you haven't done any of the things that normal people do."

"Oh, so now I'm not normal! Who is normal?"

"Lisa, you know that I didn't mean it that way. But not having played hard growing up means that you have to work a little harder to get to where you want to be. Can you hang in there for one more week and we will access things from there? If you don't feel any better, then we will stop." I was able to say that because I knew that she would feel better. If I was to show her how much weight she had lost or the decrease in her measurements right now, the pain in her legs may overrule those gains."

"Okay, one more week. One more."

During the next week, it was clear that Lisa was just going through the motions during her workouts. The complaints were numerous; I don't like..., It's too hard..., How many more..." It just went on an on. Even the down time that had always been light and fun when we were just palling around hitting the heavy bag, became heavy and tense; more like it was part of the workout than a time to cool down and enjoy. Enjoy the music that was always playing in the background during the workouts; enjoy the end of a hard workout; enjoy the light conversation that went on. I started to feel sorry for myself. I hadn't realized how much I actually enjoyed training Lisa. Before this week, the workouts were light and fun, full of two friends playing the dozens and entertaining each other.

Looking back over these last two weeks it became clear that these twice-a-day workouts gave me reasons to keep going. Being off work ill and the doctors oscillating between diagnoses, it became the scare of the week: check for cancer, check for kidney trouble, liver issues, pancreas issues, etc. However, the symptoms never ended, tired all the time, blackouts from time to time, loss of appetite.

The doctors had a list a mile long of things to refrain from: don't drive, no heavy exercise, no working, no sweets, no salt, no alcohol, stay out of stressful situations. I was just surprised they didn't say stay away from sex. It was during this time that my regard for doctors sunk to an all time low. It seemed that they closely resembled used car mechanics. Try this pill. Pay me. That didn't work; try this test. Pay me. It's not that. Keep track of this. Pay me. It's not that. Try this different pill. Pay me. Oh, that didn't work. It was a vicious cycle that did not end unless you get lucky and they stumble onto the problem. The difference is that, unlike used car mechanics, doctors are dealing with a priceless piece of equipment, you.

The workouts were taking my mind off of being sick; I needed them. For the first time I felt like I needed a woman in a way that was not carnal. With my new revelation, it became clear that I needed to come up with a plan and not simply let the chips fall where they may.

Friday at six o'clock when we were supposed to have our evening workout is when I would put my plan into action. A table in the workout area, five pounds of king crab, a scale, tape measure, my journal, and a bottle of Mumms Extra Dry champagne is all I would need.

I have the door closed to the exercise room so when Lisa comes in she will not notice the table with a table cloth spread on it sitting in the middle of the floor. When she comes in, I want her to think that it's just another day - another workout. She comes in and quickly changes into a pair of sweats. When she emerges from her room, I hit her with a big smile and a simple, "It's time." I hold out the rolled up tape measure.

The look on her face says don't play with me - you know that I'm not looking forward to this.

To break the ice, I took her height first. Like a doctor examining a patient I said, "Hm still four foot eleven and a half-no change. I opened my journal and dated the next page and wrote down the measurement. Her arms were folded over her chest and the look on her face changed to a "don't mess with be boy" look.

With that look, there was nothing left to do but change the gravity of the situation. I started putting the tape around her head like I was taking a measurement for her hat size. I followed my actions by saying, "Still Big" and smiling hard. When I saw her face break its hard expression and move towards a small smile I continued. I touched the edge of her face - right around the edge of her lips - and said, "I just love that smile." She couldn't hold back any longer - I had her.

I got down to business. There was a small size decrease allover her body with the largest changes being the three-inch decrease in her waist and two-inch change in her chest size. I played up each quarter of an inch loss and when we got to the chest and waist changes, I went berserk. Lisa was not catching on to my enthusiasm. I guess the change in measurements didn't mean that much to her.

It was time for my big finish. I crossed my fingers and centered the floor scale in front of her. She was still silent as she stepped up onto the scale. The quiet in the room made the giving metal springing/creaking sound of the scale, as it gave under her weight, seem like it was echoing throughout the entire room.

I stopped breathing while the dial of the scale rocked back and forth - it seemed like an eternity. I knew that the changes that we made to Lisa's eating habits alone should have been enough to affect her weight. What if I was wrong? What if she didn't stick to the diet when she was at work? Oh my God - I started silently wishing and praying right then and there as the dial continued to move. The dial moved first fast, then a rocking motion that my eyes could not focus on, One hundred eighty- nine.

Lisa looked at me without emotion. I gave her my emotion when I jumped up from my bending position looking at the scale and grabbed her. Unlike the emotion that I had shown when I was taking her measurements, this was for real and I believe the energy transcended into Lisa. It hit her - seventeen pounds.

"Seventeen pounds and it wasn't even that hard. I can't wait until next month - I'll do at least seventeen more, then seventeen more."

She was so excited I didn't tell her that as she lost more weight it would start becoming harder to lose weight at the same rate. There was no training that night, just a quiet celebration between friends with music, crab, and champagne. I also rented Shaft, Shaft's Big Score, and Shaft in Africa. We ate, listened to music, drank champagne, and watched movies celebrating the first step, an accomplishment in a long journey. That night, I talked her into letting me pay for her to have her hair cut the next day.

Chapter 17
Getting Ready for Another Night On the Town

I had just finished the last of the water that I was forcing down when the boys came in. They were hyped about going to one of the bars at Caesar's Palace. According to them, half of the women that they had talked to that day were talking about going there. Most of the hype was coming out of Al and Daryl and not from Len so I took it all with a grain of salt. It really didn't matter to me. I have been to Vegas so many times and have basically seen it all. My main goal was to make sure that my boys had a good time. The way they came into the room like gangbusters, it seems as if they were having the time of their lives. For a change, I was starving. "Hey, guys, are you hungry?"

"We just ate Mc Donald's," Daryl informed me.

"You mean to tell me that we came all the way from Chicago to Las Vegas for you guys to eat Mc Donald's?" Some people don't know how to be on vacation, try different things, and have a relaxing good time. "Well, I'm going to order something, does anybody want anything?"

Len started rubbing his stomach and said, "All I had at Mc Donald's was some fries. I knew that we were going to eat something later."

Flipping through the room service menu, I suggested, "How about a shrimp cocktail, a nice rib eye, a baked potato, and some green beans?"

"I'm in," Len said, "Make my steak medium."

Daryl chimed in, "Dee hook me up too, but make my steak well done."

Al, never passing up a chance to rib someone, called Daryl out and said, "Daryl, I can't believe that you have any room left after two Quarter Pounders and a Diet Coke."

"You worry about what you eat and I'll worry about me! Okay!

"Hey guys, we're on vacation we don't need any confusion. Al don't worry, you can still be my nigger - even if you don't get any bigger." I was breaking the tension in the room and pointing a finger at Daryl poking fun at his weight in a light hearted way that ensured that the tension was gone. "I'm ordering the food. Al, are you in or out?

"I'm okay. If I get hungry, I'll just reach over into Daryl's plate."

I knew that it was on and that the boys would be alright. Daryl is just supersensitive about his weight.

Before the food came, I pulled Len to the side and asked him how he was doing. He told me that he was down about a thousand dollars and wanted to get it back. I told him that he might get it back but before he tried he should see the winner that I met by the pool. I gave him the 4-1-1 on Kayla the best I could from only talking with her for a few minutes. I told him that as far as I could tell, she might be the only sure thing in Vegas.

Just like I thought, he was excited to meet her. I knew that with a little company to take his mind off of things, his gambling days just might be over, at least for this trip. I went over to the phone and dialed her room. As I was dialing the room it hit me that her room was two floors above our room. The tower that we were in is all suites above the fiftieth floor. The higher the floor generally the suite is better. I started wondering, *how this girl was flowing? She's in a suite. Is she by herself? We need to get up there and see.*

She answered the phone on the seventh ring sounding a little out of breath.

"I was just about to hang up" ... Oh, you were in the shower and you didn't call one of us to wash your back ... I know that my call is a little early but I wanted to tell you how we were flowing tonight. Do you still want to hang? ... Were ordering food in-it should be here any minute My buddies were telling me that people are hanging out at Caesar's tonight ... After we eat we could come by your spot and scoop you. Maybe bring up a bottle of Crystal to start the night off on the right foot ... So it's just gong to be you joining us tonight or do you roll with a posse? ... No that's fine. From what I remember from down at the pool today, you are entertaining all by yourself ..."

The date was set and I hung up the phone and gave Len a thumbs-up sign and a wink. He knew what I meant. The food came and it hit me just how hungry I was. I ate like a starving man and washed the food down with a Becks from our stash in the tub in one of the bathrooms. During the day, the boys had stopped by the liquor store and got everything that we could possibly need for the next two days.

Already having my clothes laid out for the evening, I started scrutinizing everyone's attire while they were getting ready. As usual, Len's getup was sharp and classy. He had on a pair of burnt yellow wide leg slacks matched with a loose fitting silk white tee shirt and burgundy-brown Armani sandals that contrasted perfectly with his slacks. You know that your outfit is on when you have taken the time to match the color and texture of your belt with that of your shoes. His polished look worked well on a tall slender man but it might not work for someone else. If you're not careful, you can wind up looking like the ice cream man wearing all those light colors.

Al's look was a little harder. A pair of dark blue jeans that were so stiff with starch they could standup on their own. A pair of black Lucchese ostrich boots were fully working with a black leather belt and a cotton/linen blend black short sleeve shirt. It was not the laid back I'm-on-vacation look which I thought was more appropriate for Vegas. It was more of a going-to-the-club look more suited for a night on the town in Chicago.

Daryl came out with most of the gear that he had on the night before. The only change that he made was black, yellow, and red flowered Hawaiian shirt. The black pants had no crease in them and surly the white spot on the upper leg had to have escaped his notice,

"Daryl, when are you going to start getting ready?" I asked.

"What are you talking about Dee?"

"Yo man, that look is just not working. What else you got?"

"I thought we were going on vacation, not putting on a fashion show."

I didn't answer. I just started going through the closet looking for him something different to wear. A dated blue suit and dressed down clothes was what Daryl had with him. We didn't have a whole lot to work with so I called down to Housekeeping for an iron and ironing board to be sent up to the room.

While on the phone, I begged the lady to find me a new sponge and send it up with the iron. For the life of her, she could not figure out why I needed the sponge. She kept asking me, in a clearly Mexican accent, what did I need cleaned in my room? I continued to tell her that the room was fine and that all I needed was the sponge. It finally sunk in that all I wanted was a sponge and not someone to come up to clean the room. My mind was working fast and I thought I had it together when an argument broke out about the flowered Hawaiian shirt. Daryl still wanted to wear it.

The conversation went on for about a minute before Len flat out told Daryl, "You can wear it if you want to, but you are not going anywhere with me with it on."

Well said Len, I thought to myself. That was that and within thirty seconds I had my main man Tim on the phone. Tim was the manager of Avanti's, an upscale clothing store in the Forum mall area in Caesar's Palace. Over the years, some of my planned three-day trips to Vegas had turned into five or seven-day trips and Tim was kind enough to outfit me for the extra days for a price.

In time, he started sending me unique items to Chicago from his store when they went on sale. Now we are on a first name basis and it was time for me to call in a favor for buying all of those over-priced clothes. There was a knock at the door and the iron, ironing board, and sponge arrived.

"Tim, how are you? ... I need you to send me a short sleeved shirt in a soft color to match a pair of black pants ... Good but I need that in an XXL or XXXL, it doesn't matter which one. ...No I didn't gain any weight. It's not for me, and what do you mean that it might be hard? ... You don't stock a lot of large sizes! OK, take a look and I'll hold on ... Great! Cream is fine. One fifty? That's deep ... Well at least for that price you can deliver it ... Yes, the usual place, room 5603. You have my card on file, right? ... Thanks Tim, I owe you one ... I know you will. Just don't send too much stuff ... I'll talk to you soon, bye."

I took some time to show Daryl how to sponge off his black pants and press them. The trick is to get most of the moisture out of the sponge, wipe the surface of the cloth not getting it too wet. As I was looking at Daryl's handy work over his shoulder, I noticed an empty condom wrapper on the ironing board. I picked up the package and looked at Daryl. No words were required. He knew and I knew that he was caught in a lie. Rubbing his nose in it would have served no purpose.

The slacks turned out good. We took the shoe cloth from the bathroom and hit Daryl's black lace ups. It was coming together and we just needed the shirt and we were out. The shirt came and it was perfect. Daryl actually looked okay, I mean, there's only so much clothes can do.

* * *

With three bottles of Crystal in hand, the plan was for each person to enter the room, get introduced, and hand Kayla a bottle. I didn't need an introduction so I didn't have a bottle with me. Also in the plan but unknown to everyone else, was that Len would go in last and I would give him just a little more hype than everyone else. I have an agenda; no more gambling for Len.

"Len this is Kayla.. I think you guys have something in common." They both looked at me, then each other. Len looked back at me and winked. We were on the same page and I knew that Len could close. One of the bottles of champagne was opened almost immediately upon entering the room. The mood in the room was very upbeat, just friends being friends, talking about life. It's great when you know that someone has your back. These guys have my back and I have theirs.

The reflection reminded me of a lesson that my grandfather taught me back in the day. No matter what, treat people with dignity.

Dee, do you see that man over there? I think that he's about ninety-one years old. He's old and broken down, a hollow of the man that he used to be; broken and hobbling across the street, but still proud. I have no idea what happened to make him lame. Maybe it's just old age, I don't know. What I do know is that he is as proud today as he was the first time that I saw him. If you were to go over there right now and try to help him across the street he would push you away and tell you that he doesn't need any help. Yes, a proud man. If you really wanted to help him across the street, it might be better to just ask him to come across the street with you to talk about the weather. You'd have left him a little something. He's letting you help him across the street so that he can help you. It is a give and take situation. Dee, friends are hard to come by. You're lucky if you have three or four good friends in your entire life. Treat your friends with dignity and they will always be your friends.

That advice allows me to try and handle the everyday issues that my friends have. We didn't strip Daryl of his manhood when we got his gear in order. Likewise, getting Len way from gambling by introducing him to Kayla does so in a way that doesn't confront him and strip him of his self respect. Besides it was the right thing to do.

Helping his boys have a good time made Dee remember the one time that he wanted to help but couldn't. A few years back, he wanted to reach out and help his mother but couldn't.

Chapter 18
A look into Dee's Past to Understand The Future

The train was taking its sweet time. For two days Dee had been bumped around and waking up in the train terminals of strange towns for short layovers on his way from Chicago's Union Station to points west. Points that led to a reunion with his mother. Six years of boarding school, then summers in Oklahoma, and back to boarding school. This, his fifteenth summer, was a break in the year-round routine that had become Dee's life. More importantly, it promised to answer the unanswered why's. The reunion will reunite him with a mother that he had not really known since the endless nights that he spent crying. Crying first for a father lost at sea after being swept overboard while trying to save a shipmate. The government's award of a Silver Star did nothing to appease the family loss. Soon thereafter, Dee was crying for a mother whose pride would not let her stay in a father-in-law's home with his son being gone.

It was no secret that the main reason that Frank stayed in the Navy, during these times of conflict, was to support the needs, wants, and desires of his family. It was also clear that Miller wanted his son home. Miller's opinion was that the money that his son was sending back should be saved and not spent on high priced new outfits or other trivial things. Saving this money would allow his son to give up his wartime occupation that could take his life at any time; Miller was very vocal on this issue.

When the telegram came, no one had to open it to know its contents. Its arrival had been foretold by Miller's constant badgering of Zephyr about her spending habits, and whether she had asked himto come home. He kept up a constant dialog of, "You know that the longer he stays in the military the more chance he has of getting hurt." With this backdrop, Zephyr carried the entire weight of the hero's death on her narrow shoulders.

Many things between family members do not have to be verbalized. They are said through unspoken looks. Looks that have a meaning that is as clear as words spoken through a loudspeaker. Looks that cause discomfort like someone is holding a knife to your back with the full intent to use it. Not to kill, but to wound a spirit that was already broken.

It was that invisible knife that forced her to act in such an unnatural way and with unnatural reason. It allowed a mother to leave

Miller's house with no decided destination. With her way uncertain and only enough money for one, she thought it best to leave young Dee with his grandfather.

Much like the contempt that Miller had developed for her, his affection for this grandchild was unflinching. Patient with the child to a fault, it wasn't long before he had grounded the boy with the fundamentals of young manhood. Zephyr knew that Dee would be fine right there; at least until things got settled with a roof over her head and a job. There would be no hard goodbyes. "Miller, make sure you tell that boy that I'll be back for him! was her command.

"You just go ahead and do what it is that you need to do Zephyr Lu. Dee will be fine right here."

She turned away and got on the bi-weekly bus headed for Tulsa, Oklahoma. When Dee was told that his mother had gone away for a while, there were tears; uncontrollable tears that worried Miller. Miller's reaction was to have Dee write his mother a letter letting her know how he felt. Dee did just that.

July 14,

Dear Mommy,

Where did you go? I miss you so much. Please come back to get me. I will be very good. Can I go with you? I can work and get a job and work real hard.

Dee

With the letter being written, Miller told Dee that he had to stop crying in order for there to be a response to his letter. He wasn't sure when the response to the letter would come, with the mail and all, but it would come. Until it did, he had to be a man and stop crying. "Can you do that for me, Dee?"

"Yes Grandfather." With that, there were no more tears. There were postcards and letters; however, there were no return addresses, just postmarks from points west: Arizona, Las Vegas, Los Angeles.

* * *

The train pulled into the station on time at 6:46 p.m. At 7:30 p.m. there was still no one. Did I get the time wrong? At 8:05 p.m., I saw a woman approaching. She was much shorter than I remembered or imagined, and she had clearly put on some weight, but it was still Moms. I was nervous as she started coming closer. It has been over six years since I had seen her.

"Hi honey! Sorry I'm late; it's this damn L.A. traffic. Come on, hurry up because Bill will be worried about where I am. He watches me like a hawk. I'm over here in the No Parking Zone."

No hug. No embrace at all. Not exactly what I was expecting after six years. Maybe after two days on a train, my expectations were just a little too high. In the car she explained to me that her life had changed. She was married to Bill Q and I had a little brother named Bill Jr. Who was four years old. I was also informed that my step dad knew nothing about me. I was being explained as a distant cousin. I wasn't given a choice. It was just the way that it was.

Emotionally, I was on a roller coaster. No matter how I thought about it, my mother was denying me. I wanted so much to please her that I didn't even think about it.

"Please, Dee, do this for me and your little brother," was her plea. Those words echoed through my mind like a song you hum while shaving that stays with you all day. That phrase, spoken over twenty years ago, stays with me almost every day. Some days it's like elevator music that's there but that can be put out of your mind. Other days it's like the bass line in a gangster rap record that wont end.

“Please, Dee, do this for me and your little brother.” A child of fourteen wanting so to please of course I said okay. I couldn't help thinking how things might have changed if I'd had the backbone to just say no.

We pulled up to the house, should I say apartment, and I was shocked out of my mind. I don't know what I expected. I do know that I didn't expect this. It was a one bedroom garden apartment in Englewood. The apartment was designed for one however, it was accommodating three.

The gold carpet in the entranceway and living room of the apartment was worn thread thin in most places. The carpet was so dirty that dust rose from it when you walked over it. An old couch, a chair, and a Sony large screen television were the only things in the room. I do remember a cable TV box and how crystal clear the TV picture was. Everything else in the room was a haze to me.

This was a nightmare but I was willing as long as Moms was willing. I was starving and I had a little over two hundred dollars from my social security benefits that I get because of my father. I offered to buy dinner. With the offer came the first interaction with Bill. "Boy, you're a big man coming in here offering like that. How much money you got boy?"

My spider senses started tingling from the way that he talked to me and I knew that he didn't mean me any good. My response was appropriate. I poked my chest out and told him, "Twenty-two dollars, more than enough to get a family size pizza."

"Give it to me."

“What!” I expected something, but not a response like "give it to me." Not wanting to reach into my pocket and pullout more than twenty dollars, I told him, "It's in my suitcase." Rumbling through my suitcase, I was able to sneak twenty-two dollars out of my pocket and close my suitcase. Now I had to sell it. "This is all the money that I have so I can't give it to you."

"Give me that money boy!"

I look over at my mother for her to intercede. She just stayed a comfortable distance away from the action shaking her head. The look on her face was almost like she was telling me to do it because there was nothing she could do. Inside of me, I was begging my mother to come to my aid. No such luck. Disappointed, a tear started to fall from my eye. Not the tears of yearning from six years ago, but tears of a child tearing himself from the ties that bind.

To stay bound would risk being dragged down a road that I could never recover from. It's a love lost, the love that you gave up because you knew that you had to for the good of everyone involved. Yes, I handed him that twenty dollars. Defiantly, I kept two dollars. Grandfather taught me to never spend or give away your last dollar. I would not let this man think that he busted me that he took my last dime because he could.

As Bill took the twenty dollars, he informed me, "Look, this buys you a week. By then you need a job so that you can help pay the rent around here."

Before he got the words out, I knew that I was in for another two days on the train. This summer I would not go and lean on my grandfather. I went back to school, summer school. Not that I wanted to go back to school, I just had nothing else. I had been emotionally shaken and I would never be the same. I matured more in those six hours with my mother than in the six years since she left Oklahoma. I had to look out for myself or get trampled. Even my mother could not help me.

Chapter 19
The Parties On; or is it?

In Kayla's suite, I personally opened the second bottle of Crystal. No one there knew how much I really needed it. I wanted to just be free, free and out of control for a change. I was tired of being the one under control and taking care of whatever issues came up for whomever they came up for. For the rest of the night, I was going to be worry free and my new friend was going to help me do it.

My friend, Mr. Crystal, was up to the task I'm sure of it. Carrying the champagne bottle around the room, I must have looked like a big former thug. By the time I sat down on the couch not so much because I wanted to but more of because I needed to, the bubbles in the fluid were starting to loosen me up a bit. I was three quarters of the way through the bottle when everyone started to get ready to go to Caesar's.

When I stood up from sitting on the couch, it hit me that I was not alright. My body, the one that I had taken such good care of, was reacting to the abuse I had been putting it through over the last few hours. Luckily, I made it into the bathroom of the suite. I closed the door and the champagne, beer, steak, green beans, and shrimp that I had gorged myself on earlier that evening, propelled from my mouth. After three heaves into the bathroom's toilet, I was feeling much better and thought that I might be over the hump and able to continue the night's activities.

As I stood up from my praying to the porcelain god, my stomach turned and I doubled over. Four dry heaves made it clear that I was through for the night.

Al made sure that I got downstairs to the suite without incident. On the way there, everything I saw, everything I said, and everything I did was super funny to me. When we got to the suite door, Al asked me a question. "Dee, what are we doing here? Why did you ask us all to come here with you now?" When Al asked me that question, I immediately sobered up. My relief from issues was over.

* * *

I've known Al since freshman year of high school. It was biology class and we were lab partners. A time for rebellion for both of us, we went to class because we had to. Studying what we were supposed to was a different story; we didn't study at all and our grades reflected it.

Don't get me wrong, we liked biology and the lab. It was there that you got to cut open frogs and other small animals. It was also the first time you did a proof where you prove your theories. It was a lot of fun, but not as much fun as being a mess-up. Thinking back over it now, I am certain that we were some of the brightest kids in the class. It's hard work trying to scheme ways not to do work, get by, and have more fun than the rules allow. You can guess that after our first year of high school, we were both at the bottom of the class. Believe it or not we never failed a class. We did just enough to get by.

How can I say that we were smart? Well, it takes so much more intellect to break the rules than it does to follow them. We were breaking every rule and finding reasons why the rules didn't apply to us. We didn't do anything bad like criminal activities; it was just kids play, but always on top of our game. By our junior year we were card carrying union members at the local grocery store.

We were sixteen but they thought we were eighteen thanks to a little copier magic with copies of our birth certificates. We were earning a man's wage at sixteen, due to our forty-plus hour work week. Additionally, I was still collecting a monthly social security check. With more money then any sixteen year old kid should have, I was growing up fast. In no time, we graduated from video games to fast cars and fast women. I also rediscovered school. After seeing my first semester grades my sophomore year I knew I had to do better. I tried and I did.

Al and I were inseparable. We bought cars at the same time, worked at the same grocery store, got haircuts at the same time and double dated; in essence, we learned how to be young men together. With no brother to talk to and grow up with, Al became the closest thing to a brother that I would ever have. Many think that blood is thicker than water. However, common experiences and goals help make-up for the lack of blood lineage.

I don't know how it is for everyone else, but for me, after losing my mother and brother, Al had stood the test of being there and has shot holes in that blood-water thing.

After coasting through the first two years of high school, it was mathematically impossible for me to break into the top half of my class. Being a National Merit Finalist and earning a great score on my college entrance exams did not get me considered by any top colleges. There's a price to pay for everything. I was paying the price for years of not studying.

Al and I both paid the price. Al never graduated from college after going to a party school, Illinois State University. For me, those two wasted years meant that I would never reach my full potential. Never.

Al works for UPS now as a truck driver who bought company stock at the right time and is living a comfortable life. If it was not for three kids, that he has to support, he could most likely retire at a young age. Again, the decisions that he made in the past were haunting him.

Al bears a striking resemblance to actor Samuel L. Jackson, but at five-foot-nine inches tall he just lacks his height. An average looking man with charisma, he has become comfortable with his station in life. He is one of the few black men that I know that understands that men do not have to be in competition with each other.

I'm proud to have had his friendship for so long and would do nothing to jeopardize it. Al knows me. He has seen me with my pants down. He possesses the ties that bind our lives together.

* * *

"Dee, did you hear me! What the hell are we doing here?"

"Al, you have to wait and find out when everybody else does."

"Now you know that we go way back and you're not going to get away with that one."

“I'm not talking no matter how much you ask me."

"Okay, Dee, it's your world, but it better be good or your ass is mine.”

Chapter 20
See What Two Can Do

I woke up this morning on cloud nine. Seventeen pounds and Lisa is so happy. Last night I promised Lisa that I would take her to get her hair done. This woman had never been to a beauty shop before in her life. When it comes to Saturday morning hair, the early bird gets the worm. Being late to the shop could make getting your hair done an all day affair. I am rushing Lisa through her morning workout like forty going north to a host of complaints from her.

We arrived at Ed's Style World on the southwest side of Chicago at about 8:00 a.m. The shop does not open until 8:45 a.m. When we arrived there were already three people in line ahead of us waiting for the doors to open. Like clockwork, Ed opened the shop doors at 8:45 a.m.

The open doors didn't stop the too loud grumblings of a man who said that he had been waiting outside of the shop since 7:45 a.m. For years it has been Ed's routine to read the Saturday morning Chicago Sun-Times paper while sitting in his well worn barber's chair. The chair is the first in a line of six barber's chairs. His being the first chair in front right in plain sight no less - his relaxed reading of the paper is in clear view of the Saturday morning people waiting to get into the shop.

It's a busy person who gets up at the crack of dawn to get his hair cut; the type of person who values his time. Ed's casual reading of the morning paper for about thirty minutes, had an effect on this man like each minute that Ed sat there was somehow being stolen from him.

In fact, the few minutes Ed spent reading the paper were his. With all that said, it did not change the fact that the guy first in line was incensed. Me, I was used to it and for serenity's sake, I have grown to accept and understand it. I look at it like a pre-fight warm-up. From 8:45 a.m. to around 8:00 p.m. there will not be a second's peace in the shop.

At times there will be so many customers waiting for service that they will overflow out the door right onto the sidewalk. The day will go on with no lunch break, no excuses that my feet hurt or my legs ache. Just servicing, one customer after another each one as important in their mind as the last, without room for error. So I understand.

He opens when he says he's going to open and not a second before. I have learned to accept many of the things that I can't change, and in this case something that should not be changed.

Lisa's appointment with Carmen was not until 9:00 a.m. Seated in the waiting area, she was armed with a copy of *Ebony* and *Essence* magazines while I had a weekend edition of *USA Today*, which has a great sports section, and a *Men's Health* Magazine. We were good to go. Before we sat down I introduced Lisa to Ed. The look on Ed's face was one of surprise. He was used to the occasional female - always a hammer - accompanying me to get my hair cut. But Lisa's refinement, or lack thereof, took him aback. His eyes said everything that didn't need to be said. There are some things that are almost never said between men. Your woman is wrecked, is one of them.

I sat down feeling a feeling that I should not have been feeling but I could not help. Lisa was a friend, not a girlfriend. Even so, I still felt somewhat embarrassed with the need to explain to Ed and anyone else who might have gotten the wrong impression. I refrained. My heart said let them think what they want to, but my mind kept badgering me to explain. Torn I did nothing; I just suffered.

Ed is a slow barber. I was happy to see that one of the people in front of me was actually waiting for a different barber. By 10:00 a.m. I was finished with my hair cut. I looked over and saw a look on Lisa's face that was recalling that I rushed her to get ready on her Saturday morning to come and sit here and wait.

By this time two other customers had come in with appointments with Carmen. As I was paying for my cut, Carmen finally blew into the shop. Her arrival did not come with an explanation for being late. Carmen did arrive with a breeze that trailed her as she briskly walked in that left an unmistakable air that informed all that she thought that she was Ms. It.

Most likely, as the top stylist in the shop, she was, at least for that part of the day she was in charge of her customer's hair, Ms. It. Not much to look at, clearly her Ms. It persona could not carry over outside of the shop. Why is it that hair care people always have the worst hair? Carmen had the worst weave that I had ever seen.

Efficiently, with the help of an assistant, her other two clients were given smocks and were on their way to a good shampoo and conditioning. Carmen turned her attention to Lisa.

"Girl, when was the last time somebody did something to this?" Carmen asked while running her fingers over Lisa's tight frizzy pony tailed hair.

Lisa instinctively crossed her arms in a defensive posture and rolled her eyes at me. I took that as my cue to go over to where they were to make sure that things got off on the right foot. With a hint of sarcasm in her voice, Lisa replied, "I've never been in a hair shop before."

Lisa's causticity was matched by Carmen, with an equally sarcastically spoken, "You don't say." Again, running her hand through Lisa's hair, she continued, "What do you want me to do with this?"

From her body language, it was clear that Lisa's frustration was building. Her reply of, "I don't know you're the expert," was not going to get us anywhere. True to form, Lisa still had not given any thought to how she wanted her hair to look.

Drawing from what I learned years ago from my grandfather. People don't plan to fail, they fail to plan and from dating women since I was twelve, I stepped in and took charge. Whichever way that it went, good or bad, I was going to have to take the heat for how Lisa looked when she left this place.

I chimed in, "Her hair is fine but it has way too much curl and frizz in it. How about a mild perm to straighten all that out? A deep conditioner and a nice stylish cut:"

Lisa looked at me like I just saved her from an evil witch and Carmen asked, "How much of this does she want cut and in what style?"

I looked over at Lisa and she still had a bewildered look on her face. Also, it was becoming plain that Carmen was hating, and that she knew with a little care Lisa's hair could be a thing of beauty. All of the king's horses and all the kings men couldn't put her weave back together again.

Finally understanding, I knew how to handle Carmen. For effect I said, "Carmen you know that all this long hair is going out of style, lets get rid of it." Carmen now understanding that Lisa had no attachment to her hair that would make her think that she was better then someone else because of it, started to relax and became a different person right before our eyes. She even smiled.

I continued by suggesting, "A long bob - how about that? Make it shorter in the back right at the bottom of her neck, feathered to just below her shoulder in the front and parted down the center of her head cupping her face. Wouldn't that have kind of a slimming effect on her face and be easy to care for.

"Girl, what's your name again, Lisa? Who is this man? Is he yours or did you just borrow him?" Carmen had settled down and was playfully teasing us.

Lisa looked at me and then pondered the question before answering, "Just borrowed."

My work was over and I was on my way back to my seat. I looked over my shoulder and said to both of them, "Don't forget to do something with those eyebrows."

Over the next few hours, I kept a tab on the products that they were putting in Lisa's hair while also going through the magazines that I had. Lisa and Carmen were getting along like best friends now. At twelve o'clock we were headed down the home stretch. Carmen was curling another client's hair, so while waiting for Carmen to finish with her client, Ed did Lisa's eyebrows. It was almost one when we were finally finished. Lisa' s hair was gorgeous.

Her straight brown hair revealed natural golden highlights that were hidden by the frizz before. I drilled Carmen about how Lisa should take care of her hair.

"Stop washing your hair every day. Wrap it up at night to keep it from being allover your head in the morning. Big rollers on the ends on some nights depending on the look you're looking for, and only in a pinch - not every day you can use hot curlers," Carmen instructed.

I made sure that Lisa gave Carmen a good tip. She was going to come back so the tip would make her service good the next time she came to the shop. Carmen's assistant was given a small tip too.

Out of there at last, we headed down 87th Street toward the Dan Ryan Expressway. Before we got on the expressway, we stopped off at Chatham Beauty Supply to pick up some hot curlers and other hair care products that Carmen had suggested. Lisa's next appointment with Carmen wasn't for three weeks. Until then she would be on her own. With everything she needed for her hair purchased, we jumped on the Dan Ryan headed north towards downtown Chicago. I pulled into the Water Tower parking lot and parked. I told Lisa that there was something that I needed from Nieman Marcus on Michigan Avenue.

When we walked into the store, I purposefully walked past the Clinique cosmetic counter and asked the clerk to look at my skin. Just as I had hoped, while I was getting my skin looked at, to pass the time Lisa did the same. Sixty dollars of products later, our next stop was the MAC makeup counter where they gave suggestions of different make-up products and showed Lisa how to apply them. When the ball is rolling downhill you have to keep it rolling. Three hundred six dollars later, we were back on our way to the car.

"Hey, we forgot what you wanted to get from the store."

"I'll pick it up some other time," I said, knowing full well that there was nothing that I wanted to pickup. It really seemed that Lisa's personality had changed a little bit to fit her hair.

That Dee is something else. He forced me to get my hair cut and permed. He handled everything. If I had to do it, I wouldn't know where to start. He is really a good friend; if I could only get him off the couch and into my room. Well, one thing at a time I feel really good. I can't stop moving my hair! It feels so light and free. Wait until mama sees it, she is going to be so surprised.

I don't know what I would do without Dee. I really like him. Lately, I know that Dee has been leaning on me to keep going; I wonder if he knows how special I think he is? There's no way to break the ice without risking the balance that we have. I think we have something special, but how do we get to the next step?

"Huh?"

"What's going on over there? Are you still with us? We will be home in about five minutes."

"I was just sitting here thinking about how great today has been. How do you do it, Dee? You seem so under control all the time."

"It's my grandfather. One simple line of advice, people don't plan to fail, they fail to plan. Most times I visualize what I'm going to do before I walk into different situations. There are a bunch of if- then-else statements that are ever changing. It's hard to describe how my mind works. I do give a lot of credit to my grandfather and my being idealistic enough to take his words of advice to heart."

Chapter 21
Daryl's Colors Remain the Same

"Yeah, he's in there knocked out but, he's okay."

"Did you ask him, Al? He's drunk. I know you know."

"Daryl, look, I can't take advantage of someone when they're drunk. Anyway, as soon as I asked him about it he sobered up. You don't give him enough credit."

"Well, what do you think it is?"

"To be honest, I have no idea. The only time that it ever comes up is when you bring it up. Other than that I don't think about it. I've known Dee longer than you and he has never let me down. Whatever it is, it will be good."

"It will be good if he goes through with it – I think that he's planning on getting married. It all fits, Vegas and no waiting period to get married. He has spent a lot of time with that nerd half-white girl Lisa."

Cutting him off and liking him less and less, Al retorted, "You calling her a nerd is like the pot calling the kettle black! Why don't we just drop it? I know that I have."

"You might have but I think it's a mistake and as his friend I think we should do something about it."

"Daryl, don't start with no "we" stuff. Like I said, I have dropped the issue and think you should too. What makes you think that you know what's best for him? From the outside looking in, it seems that he always has your back. Just from this trip alone, I think that you have shown that your judgment is suspect. Don't get involved, it's a lose-lose situation. Get it through your head, he doesn't want you in his business!"

"Yeah, I hear you. How did Len get the inside track on Kayla? From the time that we got up there he was all over her. That wasn't fair."

"For all your education, you don't use you head. It was a setup from the start. Just like last night. I'm going to bed"

Chapter 22
Kayla's in Ecstasy

I've never walked so much in my life. If Len wasn't so cute, I would have been put off by how Dee just passed me on to Len. It's funny because I was getting a good vibe from Dee - then that stupid line, "I think you and Len have something in common." Well that's just how vacation romances go - here today, gone tomorrow.

Len seems nice. We went to the bar at Caesar's and it was kind of dead. Len suggested that we kick it down the strip to see if we could find something better. When he used that phrase "kick it", I almost said no. I didn't have anything else to do so why not go?

It was still kind of warm outside so our walk was done slowly. We took in the pirate show at Treasure Island. It was a little on the childish side but all the special effects were worth seeing. Walking a little further we stopped into the car show at the Imperial Palace Casino. There were famous cars there from every era -

the limo that Kennedy was shot in, one of Elvis' Cadillacs, and many more.

The lights on the strip were great and each casino had its own theme. My favorite, being from New York, was the New York New York Casino. As great as the sites were, Len's calm way and depth of conversation equally impressed me. We talked about everything. Can you believe that a Chicagoan was up to date on the New York sports scene? We ended the night eating ice cream outside of the hotel. He told me that he had been here for two days and that I was responsible for the best time that he has had. The feeling was mutual. I was very attracted to him but it was as if that side never came up.

It was already 4: 16 a.m. and we planned to meet for breakfast, and you know a girl needs her beauty sleep. I guess that I should say thanks to Dee for the introduction. I hope he's okay. He sure can't hold his liquor. He is funny as hell when he is drunk. Everything that came out of his mouth was good. His off the cuff comments made it clear that he thought that Len and I were going to hit it off big. Maybe he has a sixth sense. So far so good.

* * *

Damn, that Dee was on again. He has a good eye. Kayla was great. It was as if I was out with a friend and not someone I just met. It's four fifteen already. Let me grab some of this couch. I hope that I can sleep with those hogs that Daryl's calling over there.

Chapter 23
Another Day in the Life of ...

"Mama, I'm on my way to Las Vegas. My plane takes off at 7 :07 and I'm just calling you so that you will know where I am and that it's my plan to marry Dee. I'll see you when I get back, okay?" I knew that Mama would not answer the phone this early in the morning. Well, I just couldn't face her and her condemning everything that I do with Dee for no reason at all. I've got thirty-six minutes until the flight - I think I'll get me some dark roast coffee.

* * *

Today's the big day. I've got to be at the airport by 8:30, Daryl thought while going over his plan in his head.

"Daryl, where in the world are you going with that Hawaiian shirt on? Didn't we just go through this yesterday?"

"Errrrr. Um... Dee, what are you doing up? How are you feeling? You know that you were ripped last night?"

"Don't try to change the subject. That shirt, why? Today we are going to the mall. There's one right down the street. At twelve o'clock, after I get some sun, I'm going to pick you up right here. You got it?"

"Yeah, Dee, that's cool. Twelve o'clock. I've got to run and meet up with this girl that I hooked up with last night."

"Oh, you got lucky last night, huh?"

"Not really, Dee. You know how we flow. I just met someone that's all."

"Okay, I won't hold you. Remember, noon. That's noon Vegas time. We're not going to go through what we went through last night with you again."

* * *

"Hey, Dee. What happened to my phone call last night? ... So you're having fun? I wish I could have been there. As much as I have seen you drink, I have never seen you drunk ... That is so nasty - you must be hungry this morning. You know that you're going to need all of your strength for Saturday? .... Do I need to change my plans and get there a day early to make sure that you are taking care of yourself? You know I will ... Do you promise? ... You got me a single room with Charlotte. You mean that I can't stay with you and the boys? ... I'm crushed. I can't wait to get there ... Okay, there will be a car waiting for us. You sure know how to make a girl feel special ... I'll call you when I get to the hotel ... I love you ... hush boy; you know what I mean. Be good now. Bye."

It's funny how talking on the phone is so different from talking with him in person. It's not that I don't like talking with him on the phone; in person is so much better. While talking with Dee, over the phone just now, I could imagine the gestures that his hands must have been making while talking to me. He has it bad, the more intense the conversation, the more his hands are moving. It would be different if they were just moving and not saying anything but the hands are augmenting the feeling of the words that he is saying. They seem to be attached to his heart. I find that when they move, what he is saying is truly coming from deep within his heart.

Before Dee called, I just finished my workout. Even then I could hear him urging me not to quit. It's like a little voice that he has put there that keeps me going long after I want to stop exercising. The voice is there saying things like, "Don't quit on me, you're halfway there, or, just three more, two more, make this last one count."

After hearing it at least once a day for the last, oh, twenty months, it kind of gets embedded in you. It's there and he's there. Well, the last three years either continues or ends on Saturday and there's nothing that I can do about it. It's in God's hands. I've prayed about it over the last two weeks almost every day and all I know for sure is that it's out of my hands.

* * *

"The doctor said that she didn't suffer. That the effects of the heroin over the years had just taken their toll on her, and her body just shut down. Would it have been different if I would have stayed? I walked out of her apartment, out of her life, only thinking about me. At the time, I didn't know that a grownup could need a kid, their kid, to pull them out of a situation. I just didn't know how to. How to be a good son. How to give all of me even when it meant risking everything. I chose to save myself. In just two years after I ran from California she is gone. Grandfather says that it's not my fault, but I can't shake the feeling that I could have helped. It's my burden to bear.

September 21

Dear Mama,
I'm sorry that I wasn't a better son. I tried but there was no base. Nothing to let me know that you needed me as much as I needed you. I didn't walk out on you because of you. I just couldn't stand not being wanted by my mother. I left without telling you that I love you. Mommy, I do love you - I can only hope that somehow you know that.

Dee

Chapter 24
Charity Gets to Vegas

That girl knows that I don't answer no phone at seven o'clock in the morning. She just didn't want to talk to me. Dammit, for the last four years I have done my best to do something without facing the facts myself. I just can't let this happen. God can't want this to happen.

* * *

“Hey, Charity," Daryl was saying his greetings as she deplaned and was nearly out of the gateway. "Girl, you look good enough to eat. Are you sure you want to go after Dee? You know I'm available."

"Daryl."

"You can't blame a guy for trying."

"Daryl!"

"Just kidding, girl,” Daryl said thinking of the activities of two nights ago while reaching for her carry-on bag.

The other night had somehow changed him. No longer was he able to look at a great looking woman and accept that they were just out of his reach. All day yesterday and even a couple of times already today, he had found himself longing for many of the above average looking women that came his way. Unfortunately, they didn't react as he expected to the lines that he used to try and get their attention. The few times in the past that he felt this way, it had always been for a particular girl. This time, he found himself approaching women of all shapes, sizes, and races.

"It has to be more than just the other night," was Daryl's only thought. Was it the influence that the guys were having on him since he came here or was he just plain turned out? Probably a lot of both. "I've got to get myself together and get back to the here and now," was Daryl's new thought to himself. "Huh? What did you say? Daryl snapped out of his deep thought and turned to Charity.

"I said, all I have is the carry-on so we can go straight to the hotel."

"Okay, I thought that we could take the Gray Line Bus back to the hotel."

Oh, my, God. No you don't have me on the public bus, were Charity's thoughts that ripped into Daryl and started her to wonder if this was a good idea. In an instant, her thoughts were back to a former place in time. In her mind, ideally, it would have been Dee picking her up, and riding in a bus back to the hotel would be out of the question; it would be a limo.

I can't believe how spoiled I have gotten. But damn, Daryl the stupid bus. Charity's thoughts stayed in her mind and did not come out of her mouth. She did owe Daryl for letting her know what was happening, so she wouldn't belittle his efforts to pick her up.

"Hey, Daryl, why don't I spring for a cab since you were nice enough to meet me at the airport?"

"Okay. We'll get there much quicker since we won't have to make all of those stops at each hotel along the way. Can you believe that it took me almost an hour to get here? It only took fifteen minutes to get to the hotel the other day in the limo."

It struck Charity funny that all of the cab drivers that were waiting outside of their cabs to pick up passengers at the airport were white. Not just white men either; a fair number of them were women. This was a sharp contrast to the racial rainbow of drivers that drove cabs in Chicago that rarely included a white dot among them, not to mention a woman.

Getting into a cab at one of the airport cab stands was even more particular since the cab driver was very polite and considerate. They actually seemed happy that you decided to visit their city. Moreover, their command of the English language was refreshing. She was use to the cab driver having an attitude as if he did you a favor by picking you up and the fare that he would receive would not begin to compensate him for the ride in his golden cab.

It wasn't a limo, but at least it was cool in the cab. The air conditioner was on full blast, calling Charity's attention, for the first time, to the over ninety degree early morning heat that had already developed.

Hearing Daryl inform the driver that we wanted to go to the Flamingo flashed her mind back to a trip to Vegas that she and Dee took over three years ago. Back then they too had stayed at the Flamingo.

* * *

After a hectic flight and getting to the hotel after ten o'clock p.m. local time, we decided to hit the bed and hit the streets the following day. As I started taking off my clothes, I remember thinking that Dee was going to be out of his league tonight because I was body by Victoria, Victoria's Secret, that is. Would you believe that he didn't even notice me? It was a great equalizer. Just ignore her and what she has on to make her feel like nothing. I bet he thought that I was going to come to him. Fat chance. I'd rather go to sleep horny, or if push came to shove, I could always resort to pleas... Well, you get my drift.

Needless to say, it was best for me to get in the shower and cool off. I showered, powdered, and cloaked myself in a black silk cover-up looking forward to the relief from my condition that sleep would bring. Expectation can be as frustrating as starting something and not being able to finish it.

While I was in the shower, I heard room service deliver something. When I entered the room there was only a small night stand light on and Dee was getting ready for bed. Almost in one motion, I jumped deep under the bed covers to a place where I would be safe from my body's desires and no one would find me.

It's bad when someone knows what you're going to do before you even do it. I set myself up by being too predicable. In the bed I settled into cold, wet, and slimy when it should have been warm, snug, and cozy. I was in a world of whipped cream. Dee, seeing my face go from contentment, to wonder, to full surprise, was looking at me and cracking up.

"What's wrong baby?" He was cracking up with laughter.

I jumped up, pulled the covers back and saw it. It's hard to reconcile the three emotions that hit me at the same time - anger, disbelief, and humor - into a coherent response so I just put my face in my hands and sat there in unbelief of what just happened. I had been whip creamed.

"I'm sorry baby. It was suppose to be a surprise," he said through more laughter. "Let me help you clean up."

Dee came to me with a towel and started wiping me off. If you have ever felt whipped cream on your body, then you know that nothing is going to get rid of the sticky feeling but a shower or bath. The wiping was of no use. If he thought that I was going to be the only one sticky tonight, he had another think coming. He kept rubbing at the wet spots on my skin with the towel and his warm tongue while I looked around the room for something to get revenge with.

Room service had brought up three bowls of strawberries and two cans of whipped cream. With my plan in full mental effect, I relax and enjoy Dee for a moment. I purposely gave off a slow moan that I knew would make his defenses go down.

"How about a back rub?" I asked him while I acted like bygones were bygones. On the dry side of one of the two queen-size beds in the room, Dee is on his stomach. I lick his back from his waist to the back of his neck and then breathed air across it. He shuddered at the sensation. He was ready. I reached over and grasped a handful of strawberries and squashed them between my fingers. I let the juice drip through my hands and onto Dee's back. At this point he must have thought it was some lotion or oil hitting his back in drops; he had no idea what was to come.

I was sitting on his rump with the obvious intent to provide him with a loving back rub. I was about to reveal my not so obvious intent to get him back for the whipped cream incident. He had one coming for the incident that made me lose my shower and become a sticky body. I was full of the closely related emotions of passion and revenge.

In one motion Dee had a back filled with mashed strawberries being worked into him. “Oh, it's like that huh," was his response.

"Yeah, baby just sit back and enjoy." I invented the strawberry back rub that night. After Dee knew that he had been had, he relaxed and let me have my way. After a few minutes of the strawberries, I reached over to grab one of the cans of whipped cream. The reaching coupled with a sudden jerk by Dee made me lose my balance and fall to the floor. While falling I reached and held onto the bed sheet dragging everything on the bed to the floor with me, including Dee. With both of us on the floor intertwined in the bed sheets. That's how it started.

From the front - on the floor, from the back still on the floor, standing up - on the floor, reflected by the mirror that was attached to the dresser that stood on the floor. Yep, it was the floor that started it all. My legs wrapped around his waist, and his hands cupping my butt, leaning back against the dresser, the dresser mirror reflecting each expression of love; reflecting each thrust of passion, and each bead of sweat forming on and between our bodies.

The fever of the moment caused us to give our all to ensure that what was happening between us right then was all that it could be. We left nothing for the next moment. Our vibration caused the dresser to rock as our bodies became one. Our heat caused the image of our love to be forever invisibly embedded in a mirror that would never talk; a mirror that stood six foot by four foot unbroken. That moment, the here and now, had to give way to the future.

Chapter 25
The Plot Thickens

Okay, Charity, twelve o'clock in the lobby right by the check-in desk. Dee and I are supposed to go to the mall so I know that he will be there. Don't tell him that I told you that we were here."

"Don't worry Daryl, Dee and I have a history here. He knows that if I want to find him in Las Vegas this would be the first hotel I would look. He probably wants me to find him. Why else would he stay here?"

* * *

After getting off of the plane, Charmaine went to the first pay phone that she could find. On a mission, she dialed hotel after hotel based upon the size of the hotel's Yellow Page ad.

"... Hello .. Can you tell me if you have a Charity Johnson registered? ... No? Thank you. Goodbye." After dialing the next hotel in the phone book, "... Hello .. Can you tell me if you have a Charity Johnson registered? In your hotel ...”

Number after number was dialed until finally, “... Hello .. Can you tell me if you have a Charity Johnson registered? ... Oh, good. Can you please ring her room? ... Thank you.”

There were seven rings and still n answer. *I better get over there before I'm too late.* Out the airport door and over to a cab stand. “I need a cab to the Flamingo,” was hastily said to the cab attendant's back before he could turn around.

* * *

It only took one look by Dee to see the setup; about a second to see it and about three seconds to put it all together. Charity's waiting in the lobby for nothing, Daryl's simple excuse to get us to walk through the lobby, and the guilty look on Daryl's face that includes him not being able to look me in the eye.

I didn't want to say to Daryl what was on my mind. It would surly mean the loss of a friend. I took a deep breath and left the here and now and accepted my fate. Daryl was safe for right now.

“Hey there Charity,” I said with a smiling voice.

“Hey, Dee. I've been looking for you.”

The gleam in her eye and its accompanying smile made the entire room get brighter for me. My heart jumped and the pain in my gut, for now, was gone. For a brief moment in time- again the here and now - everything was right. Heaviness was lifted from my presence. What was lifted was heaviness that I had gotten use to towing around with me. So use to towing it that I had almost forgotten that it was even there. The moment was right but it wasn't right.

"Dee, you know I need to talk to you?"

"Yeah, I know, I know. Not here and not now." Brightening up again, "I've got to get this man some duds so that he doesn't embarrass us another night. Do you want to come with?"

"Well since I did come all this way, I must want to spend some time with you."

* * *

I've been in this lobby for over an hour and still no answer in her room. If she's with him I've got to know. I'ma call his room.

"... Who? ... No this is Al, one of Dee's friends. He went out before I came back to the room and I don't know when he will be back ... Okay, now it's clicking. You're Charity's mother. It took me a while to get it because you called her Charity, It threw me off a little ... No, I haven't seen her ... I don't see why not. An hour in the lobby is a long time. It's okay, I'm not doing anything. Come on up; the room number is 5603. Give me about five minutes so that I can make myself presentable and get myself together ... I'll see you when you get up here."

About ten minutes later she was at the door. Al needed every second of the ten minutes to jump in the shower, put on some sweats, and comb his hair.

"Come on in, Ms. Johnson. Have a seat. You know you could pass for Charity's sister." It was truly hard for him to see this woman as Charity's mother.

"Thank you. I hear that a lot."

"Well, I'm sure that Dee will be back soon. Can I get you anything, Ms. Johnson?"

"No, thank you, young man, I'm okay. One thing you can do for me is you can stop calling me Ms. Johnson. My name is Charmaine. Call me Charmaine."

"When did you get to town Ms., I mean, Charmaine?"

"Today at 12:20. I flew in on United. Can you believe it cost me one thousand fifty dollars to get here?"

"That's a lot of money. Are you sure I can't get you something? You look really nervous. I make a mean Cosmopolitan."

He was right, this had already been a trying day and she hadn't even caught up with Charity yet. Thankful that this boy allowed her to rest her tired mind and come up to the room, she hesitantly accepted AI's offer for something cool to drink. There was a lot on her mind; if only this boy would stop talking and leave me to my thoughts.

As Al was putting the final touches on the cocktail, Charmaine started thinking about her financial situation. In a rush to get on the first plane that she could, she removed her emergency money from under the carpet in her bedroom. Never one to believe in credit cards; just big businesses' way of keeping the poor dependent on the rich, thus, the emergency money was necessary to combat this emergency.

Under that carpet, there were twelve one hundred dollar bills none dated after nineteen eighty. The money was for emergencies only and for the last ten years she had never once touched the money. She put the twelve hundred dollars with the thirty nine dollars that she had in her purse and took a fast cab to the airport. Not having an airline in mind, she told the cab driver, who was of African decent, "Take me to the big airport."

The cab pulled up to terminal one, United Airlines, and she got out of the cab. The fare was twenty-one dollars and twenty cents. She handed the driver twenty-two dollars and told him to keep the change. The airline ticket, the last seat on the plane, was one thousand fifty dollars. Cab fare from Las Vegas airport, twenty-four dollars thirty cents. She handed the driver twenty-five and of course she told him to keep the change.

Now, here she sits, thousands of miles away from home with less than two hundred dollars in her pocket. *Was that even enough to get a room in this city?* She thought to herself. She started to feel uneasy. *What if she didn't find Charity?* The thought that all she had with her were the clothes on her back started flowing through her mind at a rapid pace. This day was just too much.

The first drink was finished while thinking about the day's events, as if it was straight cranberry juice designed to help her body. Al, seeing that she liked her drink, proudly refilled her glass thinking that her drinking it quickly meant that she enjoyed it. In fact, at this point, if asked, she could not tell you how the drink tasted; the issues of the day were just that intense. Still not tasting any alcohol, the second pinkish drink went down faster than the first.

"Hey, if you're going to drink like that, you better eat something, don't you think?"

In a moment, Al was suggesting and then on the phone ordering from the room service menu. Taking advantage of what he learned from his friend, he ordered a shrimp cocktail, a rib-eye, a baked potato, and green beans.

With her shoes off, a telltale sign of her age emerged. There, sitting on the side of both feet were the most developed bunions that could be imagined. Many things about one's age differ from person to person. However, the effects of a hard working aged pair of feet can't be hidden. Charmaine's feet were earned from over twenty-five years of working in the neighborhood Jewel in Oak Park.

Charmaine was getting comfortable while enjoying her meal and her fourth drink. Shoes off, three blouse buttons undone, and her skirt up high enough to reveal the top of her stockings and the clips of her garter belt. Her appearance right then made you want to see just a bit more. Her attire, including under garments, were that of a much younger woman since all of it was either gifted to her by, or belonged to, Charity.

Al had a few drinks also and he was beginning to notice Charmaine's comfort. Her comfort enhanced thoughts that Al should not have been thinking. *How old is this woman, forty? Do her panties match that garter?*

Out of respect for who she was, Al kept his monster in check. The monster being in check did not change the dog that came out to prowl. The conversation between the two became more and more personal. After the fifth drink was down, Charmaine started to reveal the nature of her visit.

"That Dee can't have my daughter. I've seen how his family works, love them and leave them. He's no good! No damn good!" Her head was now in her hands from the effects of the five drinks that were working their way through her body.

After her last outburst, the picture to Al was becoming clearer. This woman was here to meddle in his friend's business. With this revelation, Al's spirit became offensive. Upset and wanting to protect his friend, the only thing that saved Charmaine was a thought. A thought that when told to Al by Dee, was attributed to a grandfather that wanted his grandson to have an effect on those that came in contact with him. The thought: there are very few people that should have the privilege of knowing how you really feel; only very dear friends.

Charmaine was spared because Al, in the back of his heart, heard Dee's voice repeating a lesson that a grandfather from two generations ago had taught. It is really true; knowledge spreading never dies. Clearly, this woman was no friend. Not to Dee and therefore not to him.

About fifteen minutes later, she was off of her high horse and most likely reflecting on the skeletons that had fallen out of her mouth. By this time Al's monster was in full effect. Charmaine, blind sided by the monster and her lack of carnal knowledge, was easy prey.

"What are you doing?"

"I'm getting you ready for bed."

In her current state, Charmaine didn't attach the full significance of Al's answer to his actions. Her off-the-cuff response of "okay" was said in a way hat started a ball rolling with no backstop there to stop it. The full meaning of okay was never fully interpreted by the speaker.

The one eyed monster filled her up three times. There was one more for good measure that was laid between her small, soft breasts. Its coming just missed her face, due to being used three times already thus not having the force required to get past her chin.

It was all good except that on several occasions, Al thought he heard her say the name Frank. It was in the heat of battle, with a woman he just met, so Al did his best to ignore it. Really drained from the day's experiences, they fell asleep in each other's arms.

Al woke about an hour later and was instantly ashamed of what he had done. He had let the alcohol and his anger get the best of him. Trying to come to terms with his actions, his eyes were fixed on Charmaine sleeping peacefully and he asked himself again why.

Hearing people outside of the room, he slipped out of the bed and locked the door. Having someone walk in on them is the last thing that he needed right now. Looking back at Charmaine, he noticed that all of the hard edges that were in her face had faded. Sleeping there, she looked like an angel. In that instant his heart began accepting his actions and the eventual repercussions.

An hour later, there was still a suite full of people outside of the suite's bedroom door. Still drained from the release of passion and emotion, Al laid across the couch in the room and fell back into a light sleep. Still uneasy about what had happened, his sleep was uneasy and full of tossing and turning.

Charmaine was falling out of sleep not knowing where she was. She had the feeling that you get when you wake up in a place other than the one that you are used to. You start to wake up and you immediately try to remember where you are and how you got there. She felt more relaxed than she had in years.

As the memories of a few hours before began to enter her mind; she couldn't help the feeling of satisfaction that overcame her. Not mental satisfaction but a physical satisfaction that she had never felt before. One that, had she been exposed to it sooner, would have enabled her to relate to the growing pains of her daughter better.

As she moved to get out of the bed, the smell that was coming from her body reminded her of her eleven nights with Frank. "I've got to pee," she thought to herself. When her feet hit the floor, the accompanying sound that the stirring made woke Al.

"Ms. Johnson, you're awake."

"I just woke up. I told you about the Ms. Johnson stuff."

"Yeah, but "

Cutting him off she said, "There are no buts, please call me Charmaine. Ms. Johnson sounds so old."

"About sleeping with you, I don't know what..."

"You don't have to give me an apology. We're both grown. I should be thanking you. You brought something out of me that needed to come out."

The smile that came over her face when she was talking made her look like a different woman than the one that had entered the suite a few hours before. Al got up and listened at the door. He cracked it slightly, and when he didn't hear anyone out there and looked back at Charmaine's vibrant face, he said, "All clear."

"What, are you embarrassed to be seen with me?"

"No, Ms. Joh - I mean Charmaine, I was just trying to protect your virtue."

"Baby at fifty-nine there's not much virtue left to protect. Right now the most important thing is letting me get to the bathroom before it's too late."

She wrapped herself in Al's shirt and scooted past him while his mouth was still hanging open. He replayed her last statement in his head to confirm what he thought he had heard. He whispered to himself, "She said fifty-nine."

Al glanced at himself in the dresser mirror. Walking up a little closer to the mirror, Al noticed something that he had not seen before. There were two pronounced strands of gray hair coming out of his goatee. After a closer inspection of his face, he thought to himself that he had aged since leaving Chicago, or was his face revealing what he had just done with an older woman?

Al turned from the mirror as Charmaine came back into the room. He couldn't help the words that came out.

"I had no idea that you were fifty-nine."

"Does it make a difference?"

"No, but. . . "

"Look, you didn't plan this and I know that I didn't. So what will be will be. Now what do you normally do with someone after you've made them feel so beautiful?"

Charmaine's question made Al look at her again. Without thinking, "You are gorgeous," slipped from his mouth. He told her to come to him and she did.

She spent the next hour exploring his body. She felt how he said she looked. After being in his arms for a few minutes, she looked at him and said "Thank you."

Al, not understanding what he was being thanked for, just said, "You're welcome;" to the smile on her lips and the feeling that was being emitted from her.

The unasked questions were answered from both parties and now Al understood her mission. She asked for help from the person that she had just shared herself with and he vowed to help. "Let's all get together after dinner tonight and get this all on the table. I know you might not think so, but Dee is a good man. Everything's going to be okay - EGBOK. Let's leave Dee and Charity a note and go to the mall and get you some things so that you can be comfortable staying in town overnight, okay?"

Al took a shower with Charmaine. The shower didn't help. After the shower, he still smelled like her. After dressing, he wrote a vague note.

Dee,

Things are crazy.. We need to talk. If Charity is with you, don't do anything until you talk to me. Dinner at eight. I'm counting on you to be here.

Al

Chapter 26
The Cats out the Bag

It's in my mind and I can't get rid of it. Daryl is being a busy body and trying to run my business. This afternoon we did some serious shopping. I guilted Daryl into three pairs of slacks, five shirts, a pair of shoes and a matching belt. The shopping trip was finished off with some underwear. I couldn't help but think that if there was a T.J. Maxx around then we wouldn't be paying full price. Oh, well. We had a good time shopping all day. There was still a little tension in the air between the three of us. After getting back to the room, I told Charity that I would talk to her after I met up with Al. The note that he left had me a little worried about him.

* * *

After the mall, Al parted from Charmaine. Al went to meet Dee while Charmaine went to find Charity. Both Al and Charmaine were on the same mission.

Charmaine paused at Charity's door going over things in her mind before knocking. She held her breath and rapped on the room door four times.

Through the door came a faint call of "Just a minute."

Charmaine waited for what seemed like an hour during the few seconds that it took Charity to get to the room door. Deep in her thoughts and shaken by the thought of the task before her, she was deaf to the call of who is it that chimed through the door.

Charity not hearing a reply called out again, "Who is it?" Still not hearing a reply she turned and headed back deeper into the room.

Charmaine broke out of her trance and finally called out, "It's your mother."

The door flung open in an instant to a shout of, "Ma! What are you doing here?"

"I got your phone message that you didn't want me to get until it was too late. I had to come before you made a mistake that I could not fix."

"Ma, like I told you on the phone already, my mind is made up. I'm going to marry Dee if he will have me. You know very well that I love Dee and nothing that you can say here today is going to change that. I just hope that it's not too late."

"Listen girl, I know that I haven't been the best mother. If there was a book on how to be a perfect mother, I would have bought it and used it. There's not one, so I had to do the best I could. As you got older there were just certain things that I didn't know. I had no idea..."

"Oh, Ma, this has nothing to do with you. I think you did a great job. Look at me. It's only love.. Mama."

"No baby, I should have had this conversation with you a long time ago. I just didn't know how. Charity, Dee is not right for you..."

* * *

Al's insides felt more like he was going off to face the music with a bitter enemy instead of going to reason with a long-time friend. Knowing the good friend that Dee was, Al was not surprised that Dee was right there at the room door to open it before he could fully key it. Al inspected Dee's face for signs of his mood. His face had a pained but concerned look on it. If Al was not so concerned with his mission and took a real good look at Dee, it would not be hard to see that Dee had lost almost seven pounds since Tuesday.

While Al was preparing to engage his friend, he looked around the area for interlopers who might be trying to dip in on his conversation. "Hey, Dee, did you get my note?"

"Yeah, I got it. What's the problem? You know that I'm here for you."

"Have you eaten? I'm as hungry as a horse. Let's order something."

"Man, you don't leave a note like this and expect to walk in here and order food like nothing is going on," Dee replied, forcefully flipping the note over to Al. The note caught Al's eye but missed its mark and fell to the floor. "Damn the food! What the hell is going on?"

Had Dee thought about the food he probably would have eaten something. Having lost his dinner the day before to the porcelain god and being too busy to eat so far today, Dee should have been hungry.

"Settle down. So much has happened so fast. I'm just trying to make sure that I have it all together. Give me a second." Al went over to the bar and filled two water glasses full of ice and reached over and grabbed the unopened bottle of Glenlivet. "Do you remember when you tried to get me to switch from Martell to Scotch and I said no?" Al was making conversation as he displaced the air in both of the glasses with scotch. Not expecting an answer he continued. "Dee today I'm switching to your Scotch." Al handed Dee his glass and took a long draw from his glass and braced himself.

"Dee, a while ago, you told me that the Scotch would not be as hard on my body and that the hangover the next day would not be there. You said it for my own good. We're boys and you have to know that I wouldn't do anything to ever hurt you. For your own good I have to tell you that we had a visitor today looking for Charity. It was her mother. I invited her in and she was nervous so I gave her one of my infamous Cosmopolitan martinis. Dee, she drank it so fast that I thought she was an experienced drinker. Two more drinks, some food, more drinks - Dee, you have to believe me - I had no intentions. Next thing I know she started bad-mouthing you. You know my temper. One thing led to another..."

"No, you didn't hurt her did you?"

"Not like that, Dee. I had sex with her. I had sex with her and it was good."

"What!"

"I had sex with her. I'm not proud of it; it just happened. But that's not it Dee, Charmaine old me that..."

"Who is Charmaine?"

"Charity's mother, Ms. Johnson, she says that you're most likely Charity's half brother and you know that you are but are still planning to marry her anyway. Dee, you can't do that. Just the thought of it is tearing Charmaine into pieces."

"First of all, who gives a damn about what that hag..."

"Al abruptly cut into the statement and chimed in, "I do."

"You do what!"

"I care about you, her, and Charity."

Dee's eyes were physically wide open indicating his disbelief of what he was hearing. "Sit down Al and let's talk. Al, a lot has happened to me that you don't know about. Sometimes when you get bad news you have no idea how you will mentally or physically react to it. A lot of things are timing and there are a lot of people in this world that will wait for the best time to spring something on you that could break you if you're not at your best."

Dee's hands were in constant motion and he continued, "I was way down, 1 was just getting back on my feet from gambling and all. I was leaning on Charity very hard. She was my rock, my sole support. Ms. Johnson knew that and tried to snatch that foundation away. She spitefully planned her attack to break me. I haven't been the same since. No, it is not my plan to marry Charity. You know that I broke up with her and now you know why. I love her and would never do anything to hurt her. Charity and Daryl have conspired to talk me into marrying Charity.

Al, feeling relief, asked, "So what are you going to do?" "That's not up to me. Your new lover has to come clean with Charity. I was going to tell her today but our friend Daryl, being the busybody that he is, hasn't given me a moment alone with her. I'm supposed to meet with Charity when we finish here."

"Dee, Charmaine is talking to her right now. I don't know if she is going to tell her or not. I do know that she wants to stop you two from marrying so she just might tell her."

Over the next twenty minutes, Dee told Al the entire story of how Charity could be his half sister the best that he knew. He told Al there were just some things that he didn't want to confirm because they are just too painful.

"Ms. Johnson showing me Charity's birth certificate with the name Frank Carter on it broke me down enough. That, coupled with her utter dislike of me, was enough. That same day I went back to gambling, lost Charity, and started having the most vicious pain in my stomach."

Dee continued with a full explanation of why they were in Vegas. The slight tear in Al's eye confirmed that he understood. Telling him to keep things under his hat was unnecessary.

* * *

Charity told her mother that she needed some time to herself. A virgin before today. Dee, her brother. She went for a walk that was leading to nowhere. Finally, she found herself in a nearly deserted slot machine area in the casino and sat at a machine. She never played a nickel. She just sat there and cried. "How could Dee not tell me?"

Chapter 27
Dee Confronts Daryl

Deflated, I stayed in the room and waited for Charity's call. I didn't call Lisa like I knew I should have. It's hard to talk to one woman when your mind's on another. The only people in the suite were Daryl and I. Len was hanging with Kayla tonight. Over the last two days all of Len's time was spent with her.

Al, before he left, asked me if I was okay with him showing Charmaine some of the Vegas sites. I told him, "If you can sleep with her, I can eat with her." In other words, do what you want to. I didn't like that woman and I wasn't going to start acting like I did just because she slung some sex my friend's way.

From the time Daryl came back to the room until now, I have been giving him the cold shoulder. It was cold enough for him to get my point. I didn't have to say anything to let him know that I didn't want to be bothered with no sellout.

Not having anything else to do and not being the type of person to go out by himself, he was in the bedroom watching a rented movie. At midnight it was clear to me that Charity was not going to call. By this time I had come to terms with today's events and chalked it all up to life. I went into the room to talk to Daryl.

"Yo, Daryl, you know you should not have invited Charity here."

"Yeah, but I was just taking..."

“No ifs, ands, buts or maybes, about it, you have to stay out of other people's business. Trust is a hard thing to get back once you have lost it. I think you have lost a little something today."

"Would a simple 'I'm sorry” help Dee? I'm just not like you guys. I'm not all polished and mistake-free like you and those other guys."

"Look, I wouldn't have asked you to come if you weren't close to me. You're one of my best friends. I know that friends accept friends for who they are; faults and all. Over the years you have accepted me no matter what. That means a lot to me. Daryl can you do me a really big favor tomorrow?"

"What do you need, Dee?"

"I want to get everyone together tomorrow for dinner. I really need your help in getting everyone together. I need Al, Charity, Len, Lisa, and you to meet me in the lobby of the hotel tomorrow at five o'clock. I have ordered two limos to pick us up and take us to a great restaurant. Daryl this is very important to me. Can you do that for me?"

"Yes, Dee. No problem. What about when people want to bring other people? You know that Len is hanging tough with Kayla and who knows who else might be hooked up by then."

"I don't care who else comes as long as the others are there."

"Consider it done, Dee."

"Let's go get something to eat. I'm starving."

I was hungry and my head was beginning to swim from the lack of food. I had not had anything to eat all day. There wasn't a whole lot open that was close to the hotel so we settled into a greasy spoon that had a big sign that read the best chili in Nevada. We sat down and had two bowls of the chili and two Mountain Dews. The chili was good and hot. Just a little hot for my constitution. I added some crackers to calm down the heat and very quickly ate half of the very large bowl and drank all of the Mountain Dew.

After the meal, which Daryl finished off, we headed to the hotel's casino. For the first time in over two years, I felt the urge to gamble. The rest of the trip was a gamble and if things went wrong it would not matter anyway.

I have given up on all of the games except Craps. It's a fast pace game that you either win big at or you lose very quickly. If you are at a craps table and you see a guy inching money out of his pocket a little at a time, that's someone who is most often going to lose. Craps takes balls. Either you have the stomach for it or you don't.

We found a ten dollar table and I immediately got into character and fall back into form. It's as if I had just been there hours before. It comes back so fast. I begin to tell Daryl that he is at the table for dressing only and the only bets that he is to make are for the table minimum. He is there to be a cow, to shuttle money over to the cage. I give the pit boss my drivers' license and players card and order a two thousand dollar marker. I sign for the cash and make a bet before the pit boss leaves.

The point is eight so I place a bet of three twenty in. That bet puts one hundred dollars on the five and nine and one hundred and twenty dollars on the eight. Each time one of those numbers hit, before seven rolls, it will pay one hundred forty dollars. The pit boss marks down my bet and walks away. The dice roll and the number is six easy. I get paid the one hundred forty dollars and I take the six down to twelve dollars.

By altering my bet, my exposure is only seventy-two dollars, but I still look like a wheel to the people tracking my bets. I look around the table and see that there are two other players playing with one hundred dollar chips. As such, it will be harder for the bosses to track how many one hundred dollar chips that I have.

The next roll is ten. I don't have any money on that number so I don' get paid. The next number thrown is seven and they rake in all of the money on the table. So far I have lost seventy-two dollars. I take all of my black one hundred dollar chips out of my tray, six hundred dollars, and tell Daryl to go cash it in.

That leaves me two five hundred dollar purple chips and three hundred dollars in green chips.

The next point is four. I place a bet of six forty up. That's two hundred dollars on the five and two hundred forty on the six and eight. I also place a ten dollar come bet. The first number is nine. I don't have any money on it but my come bet moves there. I decline odds and place another ten dollar come bet.

The next number is eight. My come bet moves. I tell the dealer down with ten that means take my bet down and give me ten dollar odds. That leaves me one hundred fifty dollars exposure for this roll and still down seventy-two for the last. The next number is five for which I am paid two hundred eighty dollars. Fifty eight dollars to the good and I slip six more black chips into my pocket. That leaves eight hundred fifty eight dollars in my tray and I still have action on the table.

Daryl comes back to the table and I give him a black one hundred dollar chip. I tell him to bet it any way that he wants. After about three minutes in which I make over a thousand dollars he decides to place the chip on the hard six, which pays nine to one. Two numbers later it hits and Daryl has a fit. "Nine hundred dollars and still up to win," were the stick man's comments while taping his stick in front of Daryl as the dealer was handing him his money.

When you're on you're on. During the next hour there were only two shooters at the table. I have fifteen thousand dollars of their money and there is no way that I can hide it. Oh well, after a day like today I think that God was just looking out for me. Daryl wanted to stay.

I got my six hundred dollars from him and said my goodbyes and tipped the dealers at the table a black chip. I was worn out and had to call it a night.

Chapter 28
Lisa Needs to Get to Vegas

"Charlotte come on, hurry up! The plane leaves in twenty minutes from all the way down at gate H19 - almost the last gate," Lisa screamed. Lisa had worn her most comfortable shoes to the airport. Her four foot eleven and a half inch frame did not take very well to high heels. They did give her added height, but they made her legs tire easily.

Carrying a fit one hundred fourteen pounds on a frame that, in the pass, had held as much as two hundred nine pounds, Lisa was and looked fit and trim. Today she didn't need the added liability of a pair of heels, even if they were low heels, and especially when there was no one here to impress. A pair of blue and tan two-tone Hush Puppies would do just fine to accent her loose fitting navy blue Evon Picone pants suit. With comfort in mind, she was ready to take on the world and this flight.

Her job at the accounting firm requires her to travel once or twice a month. As such, airports and their associated hassles are nothing new to her but clearly something that she could do without. Today, of all days, to make matters worse, Charlotte has already started sight seeing and we haven't even boarded the plane yet. She is just signifying and carrying on about everybody that crosses our paths.

"Girl, did you see that lady over there? She's carrying her clothes in a dry cleaner's bag. How tacky can you get?"

No matter how busy you are you can't help but look over at the person that she is pointing out and waste more time. I love her to death but sometimes that girl can work my last nerve. "We've got to hurry, Charlotte, or we're going to miss that plane," I pushed her forward towards the gate with my voice.

We got settled into our seats on the plane. It was almost a full flight, so the check-in clerk had given our confirmed seat assignments away and we had to settle for what seats they had left. I was in seat 24C while Charlotte was seated in 10B. Poor Charlotte. When on a crowded flight, the best seat is an aisle seat where you can find relief; relief from the tight quarters and the person next to you, by taking advantage of the extra room in the airplane's aisle. The next best is the window seat where you can at least lean into the planes body and find a little relief. In the middle seat, there is no place to go. You are at the mercy of the people seated next to you. If they are even the slightest bit oversized, on either side, there is a problem and you are in for an uncomfortable flight. Charlotte is in the middle seat and her aisle mates are a little on the large size, to say the least. She is in for a four hour flight from hell. Well, there's nothing that we can do now, so I'm going to try and get some rest.

* * *

It's hard on a brother when you wake up as tired as you were when you went to bed. It's seven o'clock and I have a few things that I have to get done. I need to get some of this cash out of my pocket before I'm tempted to give some of it back to the casino. I also want to see the casino host about an upgrade to Lisa's room. Neither she nor Charlotte has been here before so I want them to have the best of everything. I also have to buy back that two thousand dollar marker from last night before they charge one of my credit cards.

I slipped out of the room to see what was going on in the suite. The smell of feet hit me like a ton of bricks. Damn, this doesn't make any sense. The smell was so strong that it was beginning to make my stomach turn. Oh no! I ran into the bathroom and vomited from the smell. I went back into the room and called housekeeping. "Please send me up a can of Lysol spray. Can you hurry, there's a twenty dollar tip in it.

I was brushing my teeth and mouth when, in less then four minutes someone was at the door with an industrial spray disinfectant. I asked her to wait a minute. I went and got the cause of the smell, Daryl's gym shoes, and came back to the door. I looked at the woman standing there and with pleading eyes told her that her tip would be thirty dollars if she could take the shoes with her. I went back into the suite and had a field day with the spray.

Daryl and Al were still sleep while Len had not slept in the room for two days thanks to Kayla. I showered and put on a pair of oversized Tommy Hilfiger blue jean shorts, a pair of white deck shoes, and a red lightweight silk shirt. I folded in half two thousand dollars and put it in the room safe to pay for tonight's activities. That left me eleven thousand forty-nine dollars to take care of business with after I took care of the marker. I went down the elevator and straight to the cashier. In the past I might have stopped by a table and played a little bit before taking care of business. You live and you learn but sometimes you learn a little late. This time I would not repeat past mistakes.

"Hi, can I help you?" a little oriental cashier asked.

"Hello, I want to buy back a marker that I took out yesterday," I said to her while I handed her my driver's license and players card.

Already being nice, when she saw the amount of the marker she became even more animated with her displays of friendliness. Just to see the effect, I pulled out the entire wad of hundred dollar bills and counted out twenty of them.

"Is there anything else that I can do for you Mr. Carter?" she asked while handing me my receipt.

"No, that's all, Thanks."

I headed over to the casino host's office and asked for Dave Wilson. He was not there but the host that was there knowing I was one of Dave's customers, treated me like I had a million dollars of the casino's money.

"Mr. Carter what can I do for you today?"

"Sam, I have a friend that's checking into the hotel today. I would like to see about her room being comped on my card."

He looked up at me like I lost my mind as he was punching in my player's number. "Um ... Mr. Carter what is the guest's name that is arriving tonight?"

"Her name is Lisa Lewis."

"Okay, I have her reservation right here. Would you like her room next to yours, Mr. Carter? That suite, while smaller than yours, is available."

"That's fine. Is it available for Friday and Saturday?"

"Yes, you can have it for both days. Mr. Carter I am giving you the room based upon your past play here at the casino. I see that you have been here since Tuesday and today was the only time that you played with us. Will you be playing some more during your stay?"

"Yes, you know from looking at that screen that I won over ten from you guys yesterday. I know that you want some of it back. I'll give you guys a chance, at least one more. By the way, I reserved two of the hotel's limousines to take some business associates to dinner tonight. Can you do what you can for me with that?"

"Just charge it to your room, Mr. Carter, and we will adjust your bill when you check out."

"Oh, bad choice of words, but thank you, Bill. Can you tell Dave that I stopped by?"

Leaving the host's office, I took the elevator back up to the suite and I was starting to feel really good. I wanted to get my boys together and spend some of this cash that I won. I opened the door of the suite and the smell was back; not as strong this time but it was still there. Daryl and Al were sitting on the couch talking when I came in the room.

"Hey, how's it going?" I called out to them while closing the door behind me. I grabbed the can of disinfectant and sprayed Daryl's feet. He got the message and did not protest.

"What's up, Dee? I'm just over here giving your boy Daryl some advice on how to close on some of these women."

"Yeah, Daryl and I closed last night for over ten gees didn't we?"

"Naw, Dee that was you. I was just a fly on the wall, but it was good seeing all those white people clocking your money."

"Once you start playing that type of money they are going to watch your every move. Anyway, what are you guys going to do today? Daryl did you tell Al about tonight?"

"He's in but I haven't spoken with Len, and Charity said that she wanted to talk to you personally."

"Come on guys, let's get this thing together Chi-town style. AI, call up to that woman's room and get Len on the line. Tell him that his boys need to see him. If he wants to bring Kayla tell him to bring her. We're going to turn this town out all day today. I'll call Charity."

When Al replied, "Okay, Dee, let's get it started," I knew that today was going to be something special.

Al had Len on the phone. They confirmed that they would be down to our room at ten. I called Charity and she was cold but said that she would stop by the room at four o'clock, dressed to go to dinner. Everything was set and I was relaxed with the thought that I would be spending the day with those that really mattered in my life.

Len, Kayla, Al, Daryl, and I went shopping to spend freely. Most Vegas bargain hunters would never think of going to a small grungy looking pawn shop along the strip to do any serious shopping. On our way down the strip, I tell my band of friends that we're going to stop here. When I said that, you should have seen the look on their faces.

Daryl, being the pragmatist that he is, "what is in here?"

The AAA Pawn shop was set between a small novelty shop and a car rental establishment. I led by example and went into the shop. The others, feeling trapped into going in, followed my example. The entire shop had to be less than one hundred seventy-five square feet in size. The walls were lined with cheep watches and gaudy looking gold chains. There was an occasional small diamond locked away in a glass case. They weren't anything that you would want, especially not second hand.

The owner's name is Billy Bow. That's all of his name that he ever used. I am sure that there is more to it. In his business he was probably better off not being in the habit of using his full name unless he had to. I had stumbled onto the pawn shop as a customer seeking a loan. At that time, I was in desperate need of some cash since I had given all of mine away at the craps table over the last two days.

I traded every piece of jewelry that I had - a diamond ring, a Rolex watch, a very nice gold chain and a three quarter carat diamond earring stud, for fifteen hundred dollars. My watch alone was worth over ten thousand retail. The terms of the loan were three months to redeem at one hundred twenty percent interest.

The gambling bug had gotten back into me in the worst way. There were two days when I lost about seventeen thousand. As soon as I got back to the casino, the fifteen hundred soon turned into thee fifty. Over the next to days I kept building. When I quit playing, I had fifteen thousand in my pocket. I didn't get it all back, but I wasn't there to gamble. I was there to get away; to get away from a truth that had shattered my world. I was worn out. I had been gambling for five days straight. It was time for some sleep; as I said, this thing started in the most unlikely of ways.

* * *

Just six days ago, you could not have told me that I would ever come back to a casino. Charity had brought me back from the dead. Getting ready to find work after a long medical leave for emotional issues that I had been facing, I was hit from the backside with something that shocked the very fabric of my being. Just when I thought it couldn't get any worse; to add to my woes, the way that I was told was done in the most spiteful way ever.

Charity and I were talking marriage. I had been going out with her for more than two years. During this time, Ms. Johnson never said a word. All of this time she knew that what we were doing and contemplating could never be. She allowed things to progress to this point. Just when I needed Charity the most, Ms. Johnson hit me right between the eyes with, "Charity's birth certificate lists Frank Carter as her father."

My entire life at that point spun out of control. This can't be happening. Not now, not to me. Before Ms. Johnson could inhale from dropping her ton of bricks on me, I first felt this pain in the pit of my stomach. A pain that had to be addressed.

I just wanted to get away. I left Charity a note that I was going to Vegas, a place where I felt comfortable. Five days later, I'm still here, tired and broken. Believe it or not, money means nothing to me.

* * *

Billy Bow is happy to see us come through the door. I can see the dollar signs in his eyes. After I bought back my jewelry two years ago, Billy showed me the back room. It's the room with the good stuff in it. Not the trash that was out in the front room on the walls and in the cases.

Billy sold the good stuff mostly to the area jewelers that would come in once a week. After being treated to the back room and seeing the type of deals that you can get, I became a return customer and have been a customer ever since.

As we walk in the door, we're met with a question from Billy, "buying or selling?" He looks over at me and a smile crosses his face and he knows that we're buying. Mainly he knows because I took the time to call him earlier and asked him to set out some of his better things. I introduced him to everyone and told him that he was among friends. Billy brought out a few things of inferior quality and I gave him a look that asked, "What is this?"

"You can't blame a guy for trying. Can you?" He asked, already on his way over to a safe as he was talking. He brought over a case of items that were worth the stop. We all looked through the case and at all of the other items that were shown to us. Al bought a toe ring to wear with his sandals. Daryl, being the tight wad that he is, didn't even look at anything. He had money; he won last night at the table with me using my money. Kayla was just into whatever Len was doing. Al was at my side helping me pick out things.

He was the first to spot a Rolex watch that was similar to mine. I bought three watches; the Rolex, a Tag, and a Baume & Mercer. I handed Billy forty-five hundred dollars cash. He gave me a hand written receipt that I asked for just in case. You never know when something will turn up as being hot and you will need proof where you got it from.

We were saying our goodbyes and were about to walk out the door when Billy said, "wait just a minute, I've got something you should see."

We backed back into the store and the door closed. Billy took a small blue cloth bag out of his pocket. He reached into the bag and pulled out a loose princess cut diamond that was at least two carats in size.

"I can't move this in town. You know what I mean? Up in Chicago you would have no trouble getting your money out of it." Everyone's eyes were on the gem. It was throwing light from its center. The sparks it was giving off were radiating all over the place. Billy continued, "This baby is worth at least sixteen thousand - give me two and take it."

I looked at Billy, then at the stone, then back at Billy. While I was doing all of my looking, Billy took out an electronic diamond tester. The tester is designed to have its tip placed on a stone. If the stone is real, the device has a green light that lights up. If the stone is fake then the device lights up red. It was all green today.

To test the device, I placed the tip of it on the crystal of my watch. The device showed red. Having bought my share of diamonds in the past, I asked Billy if I could see the stone. As I was looking at the stone, Billy read my mind when he said, "almost colorless and a few minor flaws. That stone has some fire, doesn't it?"

I looked at Billy in his eyes and said, "Deal." I gave Billy the cash. No receipt was exchanged this time. "Thanks Billy. Good looking out."

Stopping before we walked out of the shop, I called the boys over to look at the stone. While they were all there, I handed each one a watch; Len the Tag, Daryl the Baume & Mercier, and Al the Rolex. Hey, he had seen it first.

"What's this for?" Daryl asked as if I wanted something in return from him.

"Hey, Daryl, this is how we're rolling today having as much fun as possible. My good luck is your good luck. I just hope that you can share some of your good luck with me later."

Al was the only one who really knew what was going on. He had tears in his eyes. Al grabbed me and hugged me while whispering in my ear, "Dee, this is no goodbye present. We're going to get through this."

I felt his strength and said, "Yeah man, I know you're right." I just didn't know if I could back it up.

At the mall we had fun. Without looking at us you would have thought we were teens out at the mall without our parents for the first time. I spent the rest of the money that I had on me, freely. Most of the things I bought were for Charity and a few for Lisa. I thought that it would be nice for them to receive packages once they got home. Worn out, we got back to the suite at 2:20 p.m.

Chapter 29
Lisa Makes Her Presence Known

Almost as soon as we got back to the room the phone rang. I answered the phone, "Hello."

"Hello. I thought I heard someone over there. Dee where have you been? You know that I've been waiting for you since 11:30," Lisa replied just a bit angry because I was not at the hotel when she arrived.

"We were out shopping; acting like kids and lost track of the time. I thought you would need some down time after traveling with your girl Charlotte. She did come with you didn't she?"

"She's here."

"I have planned dinner for everybody for six o'clock; meeting in the lobby at five."

"Dee, who knows so far?"

"Only Al. There were some fireworks. Everything is calm now. I'll tell you about it when I see you at dinner."

“Oh no, you won't. I'm coming over to see how you're doing right now.”

In a flash, she was knocking at the suite's door. Al got up to answer the door. Al had met Lisa a few times a few years before. "Hi, can I help you?" Al asked the small girl standing before him in the doorway.

"Al, you don't know me?" The look on his face disclosed his confusion. "I'm Lisa, Dee's friend. We hung out a few times at the Thursday jazz parties at the Shedd"

Al was shocked to see her transformation. "Yeah, I remember but you have changed. Come here and give me a hug."

"Uh-hum, a second ago you didn't know me and now you want a hug. I don't think so," she responded with a smile and a quick move around him and into the suite. After making it past Al, she turned around and implored, "Be a sweetheart, go and tell Charlotte where I am. You remember Charlotte don't you? My friend from the Shedd. Don't get tripped up again." Lisa's tone was playful and her comments were taken that way by Al.

As Lisa came through the doorway she saw Len and Kayla at the suite's wet bar. They were there sipping on Absolut and cranberry juice drinks that looked cool and refreshing. Lisa quickly said hi to Len who she also knew from attending different functions with Dee.

"Girl, you look good enough to eat," Len said with a big friendly smile that had friendship and nothing else all over it. Len got up and hugged the small girl. "Okay, now tell me how you did it?" Len asked while keeping his arm around her waist for maybe just a little too long.

"Did what? And where's Dee?"

"Dee ran into the room when you knocked. Kayla, you would not believe how much weight this girl has lost. Look at that definition," Len removed his arm from her waist and was admiring her weight loss; pointing to her arms that were defined but not too muscular. Rejoining Kayla at the bar, Len introduced Kayla. "Lisa this is my friend Kayla, my ..." Len hesitated and looked deeply at Kayla before continuing, "My girlfriend." Kayla smiled and took a hold of Len's hand to add emphasis to her obvious approval. "So come on, tell us how did you do it?"

Just as the question finished coming from Len for the third time, Daryl emerged from the bathroom. "Whew, that felt good."

Len retorted, "I hope you sprayed enough air freshener," to the room's laughter.

At that moment, Daryl's eyes became fixated on Lisa. She had rushed over to the room right in the middle of her workout. She was dressed in a hot pink and black leotard that showed onlookers her curvaceous body. With her hair pulled back, her flawless skin reflected natural facial highlights even without any makeup. Her attractiveness, still being new to her, was worn without pretense. She had no idea how she affected others, especially men. She was clearly oblivious to how she was affecting Daryl at this moment.

Len, trying to keep Daryl from putting his foot in his mouth again, was giving him the kill sign in an effort to intercede. Daryl engulfed in his newfound admiration of Lisa, missed Len's signs.

Saved by the knock on the door, Daryl's further interaction with Lisa was precluded. Al and Charlotte were coming in through the door. With the arrival of the additional people to the suite, Len took charge and introduced everyone. Special attention was paid to Daryl's re-introduction to Lisa. "Daryl this is Charlotte, Lisa's girlfriend. And you remember Lisa, Dee's good friend!"

It was clear that he got the message because he looked deflated. Charlotte, taking in the exchange between Len and Daryl, came to Daryl's aid. Knowing what it felt like to be an outcast, she walked over to him and said, "You must feel left out. Everyone here knows each other. Don't worry Big Daddy we'll break you in."

That was Charlotte, always handling the situation. Before long, the room settled into a festive atmosphere. Lisa, not forgetting her mission, slipped into the bedroom to find Dee.

Closing the door behind her she began, "Dee, I'm sorry. I didn't know that you weren't dressed. I couldn't wait to see you. What are you hiding under there? You've seen me before. Come on let's have a look." Lisa was playfully pulling at the towel around Dee's waist. She looked up and was hit hard by the somewhat hollow look of his face. "You haven't been taking care of yourself, have you?"

"I feel fine."

"You look terrible. You need to get rid of these people and get some rest. I'm telling them to leave."

"No you're not! These are my friends."

"Dee!"

"Okay, I'll make you a deal. After dinner tonight I'll get some rest. Okay?"

* * *

Charity was just about to knock on the door when Lisa and Charlotte opened it to leave the suite. Lisa knew right away who Charity was and spoke to her. "Hello, Charity."

"Hi, do I know you?"

"Not really, but Dee has spoken a great deal about you." Charlotte, not wanting to get in the middle of this potential cat fight said, "Lisa, I'll meet you in the room, okay?"

"Kay, I'll be right in." Turning her attention back to Charity she said, "Look, I don't know what you know about me but I can assure you that Dee is just my friend. My best friend. What has happened between you two is killing him."

"It's a hard time for everybody involved," Charity replied.

"Can you give me a few minutes of your time so that we can talk?"

Charity looked at the small woman who was inappropriately dressed and decided that she was sincere. Over the next forty-five minutes while Lisa got dressed for dinner, the two women brought each other up to date over the last four years of events. Both were enlightened with a better understanding of what they had gotten themselves into. In the end, each reaffirmed their commitment to Dee to the other. It was sinking in with Charity that Dee really was her brother and no matter what, she loved him.

* * *

At five o'clock my posse started to assemble in the lobby of the hotel. The sight of nine well-dressed people of color gathered together caused some to stare our way. We were dressed to the nines and I was truly happy with the suit that I had made for me just a few days before. It still draped well even with the weight loss. When Len gives you a compliment, then you know that your gear is on. The limousines pulled up and we got in them. Charmaine, Charity, Al, and Daryl were in the front car while Len, Kayla, Charlotte, Lisa and I were in the second car. The motion of the car was making me a little dizzy. I closed my eyes while Stevie Wonder's Ribbon in the Sky was playing in the background. The music was comforting and the ride short - about seven minutes. I was starting to feel the dizziness go away as we arrived at our destination.

When we arrived at the restaurant, I walked through the door and asked for the owner of the restaurant. The restaurant was named Teibel's. The menu featured steaks and seafood. The service and food here are outstanding. I had called beforehand to ensure that our table was ready. It was. The owner sat us personally. The cracked crab accompanied by the first of eight bottles of Dom Perigon Champagne was at the table in an instant. Everyone ate heartily and drank freely. Somewhere around the seventh bottle of champagne, I cleared my mind and stood up to address my friends.

"May I have your attention?" Raising my voice, it seemed that I could not get enough air inside my lungs to be able to get loud enough to get everyone's attention. On the third try I had their attention. "I want you guys to first raise your glasses to the best friends that a man could ever have. Please, raise you glasses to yourselves." They reluctantly complied and toasted.

Dee continued, "Most of you guys have known me for a long time. There's a certain way that you grow accustomed to living, a certain pace. As we get older there are things that break into that pace. For about the last five years my pace has been off, not broken, but off all the same. Things just weren't right. The only way that I was able to make it during those times was with the grace of God and you guys. So right now, I tip my glass to you all." Dee took a sip of his first drink of any kind in two days and continued, "There are a lot of things in life that throw us for loops. Most of us deal with those times with a bend-but-don't-break attitude. However, there are one or two fundamental quality of life issues that require a man to stand fast." Dee's hands were in motion adding color to his words. "Not to yield. To yield would mean to break the pace that has been his life. I face one of those crossroads in my life now.

"Guys, I'm sick, really sick. Most of the doctors are saying that it's inoperable and that I should fade away peacefully. You guys know me, that is just not acceptable. There's one doctor here in Las Vegas who has an experimental procedure. He thinks there's about a twenty percent chance that I can make it. I want to take that chance, the chance to keep my pace and not just fade away. In my life there have been too many that have influenced me and I never said thank you. Not this time. This is your formal thank you, each and every one of you, including you Ms. Johnson, for the effect that you have had on my life. One last time here's to the best friends that a man could have." Dee raised his glass and drank every bit of fluid from it and sat down quietly. The table was still for fifteen seconds that seemed like over an hour.

Feeling the room's dismay, Dee got back up. "Come on y'all. This ain't no funeral!" With that said, he signaled for the waiter to bring the last bottle of fine champagne to the table. It was uncorked and handed to him.

Dee quietly started singing. "So drink my friends, a toast to Dee. To Dee Carter, long may he be. These are words we'll always sing, a toast to Dee Carter. So drink my friends, a toast to Dee. To Dee Cart..."

After going through the verse three of four times the entire table had joined in. Len, remembering it as an adaptation of an old fraternity song, was the first to join. Everyone else followed in time. Dee took a long swallow from the bottle and passed it on to Len who did the same. Daryl followed. The biggest smile crossed Dee's lips when Ms. Johnson demanded the bottle by almost ripping it out of Kayla's hands.

Charmaine was looking at this young man and seeing a bit of the gentleness that her first love had. She not only toasted Dee but she also toasted away the lingering effects of a long past broken heart. She was whole again. She passed the bottle and smiled at Al; her mind was in the gutter.

Chapter 30
Lisa Knows What She Wants

Lisa's mind was working. She pulled Len over to the side before they got into the limos and told him, "The party's in Dee's suite and I'm taking Dee to mine so that he can get some rest. Len, please make that happen. I'm sure that Dee would like you guys to keep going and you know that Dee needs some rest."

Len's reply was, "Done deal. We have most of the things that we need in our room anyway."

As soon as he finished talking to Lisa, Len turned to Kayla who had been eavesdropping. Before he could say a word to her she began, "Don't worry baby, I got your back. I'm right here." It felt good to Len to know that she was with him.

* * *

Lisa came into Dee's suite to get something for Dee to put on and be comfortable in. It was just her luck that Charity was in the bedroom with her head in her hands. She looked up at

Lisa and said, "I want to see him - I know you've got him locked away somewhere!"

"Look, I'm no expert at this; I just want him to get some rest. Why don't you ride with us to the hospital in the morning? He needs to be there at nine. Call my room at seven. Okay?

She replied "okay" through her increasing sobs. As Lisa was leaving the room Charity called out, "Please tell him that his sister loves him."

Lisa came back into the room and hugged and kissed Cee on the cheek. "He knows that. You must know that he loved you enough to leave you when it tore..." Lisa started crying and ran from the room and out the suite's door. It was all too much.

* * *

Dee was lying across the couch no different than he had done hundreds of times before in Lisa's basement apartment. He was comfortable. Lisa threw him a package of pictures that she had gotten back from Walgreens yesterday. There were twelve pictures. The first one was of Lisa in some of her now too big clothes. The next three were of her standing inside of her outline of two years ago that Dee had drawn on the mirror. Dee yelled out to her in the bedroom, "You are so much smaller." The rest of the shots were of her working out. "We did it didn't we?"

"Yeah, Dee and Lee did it"

"Oh, hell no. You didn't go there. Come here," Dee demanded. Lisa sat on the couch at

Dee's legs waiting to be lectured. Look, Lisa, you don't have to solve my issues with Charity."

"Look, I'm Lisa. Look at me sometimes. I'm a woman, too. The last four year, no matter what I did, you never once looked at me. I have feelings." The tears were in her eyes but she wouldn't let them fall. She quickly got up and went into her room and shut the door.

A few minutes passed. Dee got up and knocked at the door. Lisa replied, "Come in." She had the covers pulled up to her neck.

I'm sorry Lee. It's just too much happening too quick. I'm trying to stay in the here and now; to let tomorrow take care of itself, but it is so hard. The last four years weren't about you; they were about me and my pains - mental and physical. I haven't thought about anything other than what was happening right then for so long. How could I ever think of a life with you?"

After a brief pause Dee continued, "Without admitting it to myself, you have been my life for a long time. A reason to live. That realization came to me today. An old man made me stop and buy something. He made me buy a future, something other than the here and now."

Dee pulled the small blue cloth pouch out of his pocket and handed it to Lee. He whispered, "If I make it, then I'm sure we will make it."

Lisa was speechless. It didn't matter that the diamond was simply gorgeous - what mattered was that the one that she had given her heart to loved her back. Not speaking for a long time, she began slowly, "I knew a long time ago when you sang "Sweet Thing" to me. Do you remember Dee? *I'm a love you anyway you are. Even if you cannot stay. I think you are the one...*"

Her voice was beautiful, raspy with a little gravel in it. Dee kissed her. A dry kiss that, if one was into the physical act, left much to be desired. A kiss that was so mentally pleasing that it lasted and lasted. As he got under the sheets with her, he noticed that her feet could use a little lotion and that she had on mismatched bra and panties. It was a good bra though. He released the bra from the front and fell asleep right there. They slept the night away.

Chapter 31
Dee Faces the Aftermath of Everything

Dee woke in the morning with a freshness that he had not experienced in the years since his breakup with Cee. The emotion of the night before was both draining and healing at the same time. It was just a bit before seven and he was not due at the hospital until nine. There were a few things that he wanted to do and he only had a short time to do them in.

While getting dressed, Dee looked over at Lisa and saw an angel lying there fast asleep. Seeing her resting so peacefully, it was hard for Dee not to wake her from her sleep. Instead he opted for a simple line scrawled on a piece of hotel letterhead.

Lisa, I didn't want to wake you - I'll be back in about an hour.

Dee

* * *

The suite was a mess. The evidence of a party that must have lasted well into the night was everywhere. Not knowing who was there, Dee quietly made his way through the suite.

On his way to the bedroom, Dee saw Daryl in plain view asleep on the couch. Al was sitting upright on the love seat across from the couch also fast asleep. Sitting there, they looked like they were frozen in time, like one of them must have been in mid-sentence, when they fell off into their current state of slumber. Dee silently amused himself briefly with the thought of Al and Daryl's conversation picking up right where it left off as they eased out of their sleep.

Dee, now at the bedroom door, entered only to be surprised at the sight of Charity sleeping restlessly on the bed. Fully clothed, she was wrapped loosely in the silk shirt that he had worn the day before while shopping. Dee thought about all the walking they had done the day before in the Vegas heat and how much he had to have sweated into the fibers of the shirt's fabric. The fact that she didn't mind the sweaty shit coupled with the sight of her sleeping there, warmed his insides.

Sister or not, his feelings for this girl were still in full effect. The last two years of separation from her had not diminished what was within him. In that instant the freshness of the feeling he had woken with was lost.

At the sight of Charity, Dee's mind started racing and searching for a way to make what was not, be. Instinctively Dee reached out to

Charity to pull the bedspread over her. At that moment, her eyes are wide open and almost instantaneously she sat up as if startled.

Her quick movement stirred the faint smell of cologne and sweat that was resting within the shirt that she was wrapped in. The smell went straight to her head bringing back memories of the past. "I knew you would come back to me. Oh Dee, I love you so much. We can make..."

The look in Dee's eyes cut her off and took the thought right out of her mouth. It was a look of not wanting to hear what he knew his heart could not take. The emotional pain of the moment was accompanied by a heartache that only one who has loved completely and lost love completely could understand. Every beat of a heart that ached took a toll on him. Then and there, his fate was sealed.

The pain within his cancerous pancreas took a hold on him, forcing him to sit on the edge of the bed next to Cee. Dee's act of sitting on the bed was taken as a positive sign by Cee and she continued. "Darling, I don't care. My heart doesn't care. I know we are meant to be. We can go away from everything and everybody and start over, makeup for lost time."

Dee smiled as he realized the amount of love this woman had for him and how she was laying it all on the line for him. A great effort to mandate an outcome. Dee started slowly and said, "Cee, I can tell you that I love you from deep within. For the last two years I've tried to get past what could not be. I will never get past the pain and shame of what I have done and how I continue to feel about you. Anything that I do to keep us together can only make things worse."

"That's not the Dee that I know talking. The Dee that I know follows his heart and gives us a chance to be happy."

The tears of love were in both of their eyes, falling freely from Dee's while being willed not to fall by Charity. Charity's tears bore a path right to her heart and were they to fall they would cause more damage to her. It would create the type of open wound that Dee had suffered from since being apart from Charity.

"Charity you know that every part of me wants..."

The sudden opening of the door interrupted his speech. Lisa stormed into the room with a shout of "Dee!"

Daryl followed Lisa into the room while Al stood in the doorway not knowing whether to stay or go. Dee quickly glanced at the door when it opened but immediately turned his head to hide the flowing tears that were steaming down his face. Not in control of anything, in the brief moment that he turned away, he regained control of himself. Getting up from the bed and clearing the phlegm from his throat he began. "I'm glad that you guys are here, I have something for each of you."

Dee walked over to the room's closet and removed five oversized envelopes from his suitcase; one for each of his friends. There was a name neatly printed on each envelope with the words "open in case of emergency" just below them. Dee gave each of his friends an envelope. He asked Al to make sure that Len got his. "Okay guys, I've got to get ready to get out of here."

"I'll wait for you next door Dee," Lisa replied.

"Dee, we will finish this conversation when you're feeling a little better," Charity said in a voice that was too loud and meant for Lisa's ears also.

Lisa answered Charity back with a roll of her eyes and followed her out of the room, out of the suite, and into the hallway. In the hallway Lisa started in on Cee. "You are so selfish. Why would you upset Dee knowing what he is facing today?"

"Just come off of it girl. You want me to disappear so that you can have your way. It's not happening."

Wanting to hurt Charity for not putting Dee's needs first, an argument that should have never started continued. Lisa threw salt at Charity and it hit hard. "I've already got him; he told me so last night when you were in the bedroom feeling sorry for yourself. So you can take your snake in the grass ass back to where you came from."

The words had their desired effect as Charity turned and started down the hallway. Catching her composure, she turned and called to Lisa, "I'll see you at the limo to go to the hospital." Resuming her walk down the hallway and turning the corner she was gone.

Chapter 32
Dee's Fate in the End

There was to be no operation that day. The health of Dee was at issue. After one look at him and a brief exam, Doctor AG broke the news to Dee. His friends were in the room for support.

"In the two weeks since I've seen Mr. Carter, his condition has deteriorated to a point that the procedure that we were contemplating would do more harm than good. We have taken x-rays and they confirm that things have spread. Frankly, I don't understand how he's tolerating the pain that he must be feeling. It is just a matter of time. I want to keep him to run a few tests overnight and do some pain management. He should be ready to go home by noon tomorrow."

* * *

In control of his pain medication and no hope for an operation to save him, Dee chose to leave with dignity. There was no need to prolong what had to be. The button to dispense the pain medication in his hand was pressed repeatedly many times after he had lost all feeling. The lack of desire to live coupled with his over medicated state made it easy for him to slip away.

* * *

Being as light as the warm dry air allowed the current to flow throughout every fiber of Dee's body and soul. The soul, having been released from the constraints of a body, was free to fulfill a destiny that a lifetime of kneading had only begun to shape. With the soul being free, all else poured from the funeral urn and floated downward from a starting place high atop Hoover Dam. The crisp stiff dry wind captured the ash sending it whirling downward to mesh and be in complete harmony with the environment. The ashes were completely unrestrained.

On close inspection, within the ashes being scattered by the wind, one could see small remains of fabric with different tones of green that had escaped the charring that the intense heat had caused. The almost undetectable color enhanced the moment by providing a hint of what once was. In the end the moment was no more than an end to what had to be and a beginning to what must be. It defined the here and now.

* * *

Not believing what had happened, Len was the last to open his envelope. The ashes being spread today was the final straw for him. Like the other envelopes Len's contained a letter saying goodbye, a copy of the will, a copy of the receipt for funeral costs, and a fifty thousand dollar insurance policy with him as the beneficiary. The most he could get without a physical exam. Dee was truly a friend to the end.